Zinnie Stokes
Zinnie Stokes

Zinnie Stokes
Zinnie Stokes

Donald R. Marshall

Deseret Book

Salt Lake City, Utah

©1984 Deseret Book Company
All rights reserved
Printed in the United States of America
Library of Congress Catalog Card Number 84-70216
ISBN 0-87747-992-5

First printing March 1984

*For
Steve,
Kay,
Dale,
and
Jon*

One

The night she died, he lingered for a long time in the falling snow. He had walked for more than two hours, the white flakes drifting down silently around him, before he finally let himself drop down onto the bench. And then, for a long while, he sat staring out into the blackness beyond the blur of white that continued to fall from the sky.

It was not as though he had had no warning, no time for preparation. And it was not as if his faith in an after-life, in the spirit's continuation beyond death, had failed him. It was something else, something he had not planned on, not bargained for. It was something connected with loneliness, with isolation, even abandonment—as if, in her going, she had suddenly, unexpectedly, taken every-thing with her; as though the world were still going on out there somewhere, wherever she was, but he was the one that had been excluded, a sudden exile in a strange land where nothing seemed quite familiar and even the snow's cold and silent descent somehow told him that he was the one who had died and that now there was nothing left to be done but cover him up and bury him . . .

He got up from the bench, the burning in his lungs urging a protest, but when he opened his mouth to cry out, there was nothing but a mute gasp followed by the silent steam of his breath. He steadied himself against a tree, and for a moment longed to thrust his weight against it, to uproot it, as if by such defiance he could halt what was happening, bring Lois back, and start over again sometime in the past before the first snow had fallen, even before the leaves had started to turn, before the cobalt treatments, the chemotherapy, the first unsettling trip to the medical center—backward in time even until some spring morning when their world had not yet splintered like a cracked lens and words like *melanoma* and *terminal* had not yet intruded on their vocabulary.

He felt someone's eyes on him and turned in time to catch a passerby who had paused to glance quickly over the shoulder of his heavy overcoat before hurrying down the path. *He probably thinks I'm drunk*, he thought. *A grown man wrestling with a tree in the middle of a park at two or three in the morning . . .*

He straightened up, blowing on his cold hands, realizing for the first time that he must have left his gloves in the car or at home. He started walking. Except for himself and the person who had just passed by and then disappeared, the park seemed empty. He was glad no one else was around; he wanted them to leave him alone. It was none of their business, and he didn't want to answer any questions or explain anything. Yet something tightened inside, forcing him to acknowledge that it was partly a lie. In a way, he *did* want to explain. He wanted them to know; he wanted, in fact, to stand up on the deserted bandstand and break the news of what had happened. Was there no one else shocked or heartbroken? Didn't anyone know or care?

Distressed by the paradox of his torn feelings, he

turned abruptly and started off on a trot down the path where the last footprints were rapidly filling with snow. His eyes and throat burned, but he ran on from one end of the park to the other, turning and sprinting along under the glare of the lights lining the park. How many times he circled the park he didn't know, but he finally found himself cutting in front of a car that honked and sprayed slush on him as it swerved, and he panted across the street and down the two long blocks to where his own car waited under a heavy covering of snow.

He caught himself mumbling words he couldn't understand as he vigorously brushed the heavy layer of white from his windshield, then scraped irritably at the stubborn glaze of ice underneath. Then, standing with his hand on the door's cold handle, he tipped back his head and looked up helplessly into the descending flakes. Before he got inside, he scooped a handful of snow from the top of the car and rubbed it on the hotness of his cheeks.

"Gavin!" he thought he heard someone call. He started to turn, then, hoping he was mistaken, ducked down to get into the car. "Gavin Terry!" the voice called again. This time there was no mistake. But he continued getting into the car and, for a moment, sat there breathing heavily on his icy fingers, leaving the car door ajar.

He heard them approaching, and suddenly they were there, two figures leaning down to look through the open door. "Gavin?" the male voice asked. He cast a quick glance up at them, wishing that he wouldn't recognize them, that he could say, "I'm sorry, but you must be mistaken—"

"Gavin?" It was Ted Walker. The Walkers: Ted and Sheila. Ted's gloved hand was on his shoulder now as his voice went on talking: "Hey, man, we thought it was you. We were just on our way home from a party and thought we saw your car—"

"How's Lois?" Sheila was saying, bending down to peer in at him.

"Everything okay?" Ted echoed, his voice sounding more hollow now and unsure.

What do you say to people—especially the first people—who ask? He looked away, but it wasn't that he feared his expression would collapse or that tears might suddenly fill his eyes; it was actually, he realized, more as if he had been pushed from the wings onto a strange theater's stage where actors repeated their lines with increasing intensity as they glared at him, expecting him to pick up some cue and carry on with a play he had never heard of.

"Is something wrong, Gavin?" Sheila asked.

"She died—a little while ago," he heard his own voice say, sounding like some strange, muffled announcement coming over a loudspeaker in a crowded air terminal.

"Oh, no!" Sheila said, and the pain in her voice made him ache inside. Ted's hand tightened on his shoulder. "Oh, Gavin," he was mumbling, "we're so sorry."

What was it going to be like? he wondered. *Going through this with all their friends, one by one—could he do it? Would he be able to face them, to bear up?*

"I guess we all knew it was—was coming sometime," Ted was saying. He had squatted down beside the open door now, his gloved hand gripping Gavin's knee. Gavin looked at them, studied their pained expressions, and watched the clouds of steam coming from their open mouths. Ted's voice went on, "It's just that—you always hope, I guess, that—"

"Right," he heard himself agree quietly, and he let his head tip back as his own breath sent a steady cloud into the frosty air.

"Oh, Gavin," Sheila whimpered. "Is there anything we can do?"

"Thanks," he breathed. "Let me think about it. Right now—"

"Where's Shawn?" Ted cut in. "Does he know yet?"

Shawn. He had thought about him off and on during the past two or three hours, always picturing him the way he had left him at home, his six-year-old shape curled up in the red-white-and-blue bed, the big Snoopy propped droopily beside him.

"No," he said weakly, dreading the moment he would have to tell him. "Not yet."

"Who's he with?" Sheila asked. "Do you want to bring him over and—"

"No, no. But thanks. Katy's with him—a lady from the Church, a friend of ours. She offered to come over if— well, if anything happened. So I called her tonight after the hospital phoned."

"Were you there? Were you in time to—"

He tried to breathe deeply. "Yeah, I was there." He swallowed. "For the last."

Gavin, he could still hear her hoarse whisper. *Sweet Gavin, you've been such a trooper . . . Such a dear.* Then she had winced with pain, and finally smiled once again: *How could I have been—so lucky? To have had you both?* She had drifted then, the smile fading to a frown, then slowly, slowly, coming back. *Love that dear little boy—for both of us.*

"I mean, was she—was she coherent?" Ted was asking.

"Oh, yeah, she—she talked. Completely rational . . ." Then his mind drifted off.

He's such a sweetheart . . . Such a dear boy. Then, for a long time, no words, just the smile and the eyes resting closed. But once again, the forehead furrowed, and he heard the pained words: *Oh, dear, I just remembered something. Something I was always going to do.* He waited, then dropped to his knees beside her and put his face close to hers. Finally he had tried to help: *What is it? What can I do?* A little silence, and then the words: *I always meant to do it. I really did.* And a sad little smile. *Please write to Mrs. Kocherhans. Remember? The la—* He interrupted her— *Yes, yes. I remember*—and she sank back into the pillow. *What can I do?* he finally asked very softly.

Suddenly he became aware of Ted's grip tightening on his knee.

"We wanted so much to go," Sheila was saying. "Just yesterday, Ted, wasn't it? Oh, I feel so bad. I intended to go." She started to cry. "I don't know why there are always these things I'm going to do, and then, somehow, I just never seem to—"

A long time ago she loaned me a book—stories from Shakespeare. I really did think I'd returned it. But then I found it—a whole year later—when we were packing to leave Cleveland. But— She seemed to wince and, for a moment, turned her head away. *I was so embarrassed,* she whispered. *And what made it worse,* she said, looking up at him, *what made it worse was that—I saw that Shawn had scribbled all over the title page with a—a blue crayon.* And she started to cry. *Don't worry,* he said. *I'll take care of it.* Her eyes again, trusting, knowing. *Please do that—for me. Get it back to her someway. It's been on my mind . . .* He nodded: *I'll send it.* He felt her hand tighten on his as she sighed and closed her eyes, smiling faintly. *Thank you,* he heard her whisper. *Just to clear the slate—*

To clear the slate.

"—could come over, if it would help at all," he could hear Ted saying.

"By all means," Sheila echoed. "You know, Gavin, that we'd do anything—"

"Yes, I know," he said. "And I do appreciate it."

Just to clear the slate. His eyes watered, and he felt a

sudden twinge as if a nerve had just been exposed or an old wound reopened. Clearing the slate: it was like something he had read about Sophocles or Socrates. How was it? Sophocles wrote plays, but Socrates was the philosopher. Socrates, then. Condemned to die—made to drink hemlock?—because he had been accused of corrupting the youth, Socrates had turned to someone and asked him to pay a debt for him: he had borrowed a chicken or a rooster from someone and hoped now that it might be returned. To clear the slate. He shifted uncomfortably. Lois had wanted a simple book returned. How much more reason did *he* have for settling old scores, paying old debts?

There was a moment of silence with only the three clouds of steam mingling in the night air. The snow had stopped falling.

"Sorry to keep you out here, pal," Ted said. "You'd better get home before you get sick."

"Don't you have gloves?" Sheila asked.

"Yeah. They're here, somewhere." He looked up at them, standing helplessly, awkwardly, as if afraid that carrying on their own lives as a couple might be painful or offensive to someone left suddenly alone.

But he wasn't alone. Shawn and the red-white-and-blue bed and the big Snoopy were still there at home, untouched, waiting unsuspectingly for him to come home and overturn their world. Or had something—some unconscious premonition, something imperceptible in the air—awakened the boy, and Katy had had to tell him? The questions flooded upon him: did he secretly hope that this was so, thus giving the burden of breaking the news to Katy and therefore sparing himself? Or did this thought make him feel cheated, robbed of an intimate ritual, poignant and unique, meant only for a father and his son? Or was it all wrong to begin with anyway, because, when the hospital had summoned him earlier that night, he had not thought to rouse Shawn from his sleep and take him to his mother's side for some last word or glimpse or kiss from her? Why hadn't he even thought of it? Would the boy one day hate him for this? Or was it better that—

He felt Ted's gloved hand squeeze his knee and saw that he had crouched down once again on the curb, his cocker-spaniel eyes, begging to be of some help, now level with his own.

"I know you've got a lot to think about, Gavin," Ted said softly. "We won't keep you. But call us if there's anything at all—"

"I will," he breathed, and Ted helped him shut the car door. Without rolling down the window, he raised his hand to them in a parting signal and saw them wave back slowly as he started the engine and pulled out into the glistening slush of the street.

The big Snoopy had tipped sideways so that one of its arms rested on the back of Shawn's neck. From the glow of the night lamp, he could see Shawn breathing heavily and regularly, oblivious of the floppy dog's casual embrace. He was glad the boy had not awakened, and he hesitated to disturb him now. Confronting Katy had been painful enough: he had tried to steel himself adequately on the way home, but entering the front room and knowing that Lois would never be there again, topped off by Katy bursting into tears, had suddenly invalidated everything, and he had wept openly.

He was thankful for Katy's help—thankful for all the Church members in the Columbus area and their willingness to help throughout the whole ordeal of Lois's illness—but he was glad that Katy had not stayed any longer than she had and that now, for the first time since he had been called away six or seven hours earlier, he was alone in his own house with Shawn sleeping peacefully before him.

Gavin dropped down noiselessly beside the bed and let one of his hands slip lightly over Shawn's own. When the boy didn't stir, he let the back of his hand run slowly along the downy smoothness of the small arm protruding from the Kung-Fu pajamas, then gently grazed the boy's neck and chin until the back of his fingers rested lightly against the softness of his cheek.

Shawn squirmed. One eye drifted halfway open, then floated shut again. Gavin pulled his hand back, not sure he really intended to rouse the boy. But he caught himself reaching out once more to rub the back of his hand against the smooth cheek, and he knew that that was exactly what he wanted.

"Shawn," he whispered. One finger traced along the boy's chin, over his upper lip, and up along his temple and forehead. "Shawn," he tried again. The boy's eyes opened reluctantly, then started to close, and Gavin bent to brush his cheek with his lips and whisper once more against his ear: "Shawn, it's Dad."

The boy blinked and started to sit up. "Is it morning?"

"No." Then catching sight of the pale blueness outside the window, he felt compelled to add: "Well, almost, I guess."

"How come you're already dressed? How come—"

He touched the boy's lips with his finger. "Shawn—"

"What's the matter?" His eyes clouded with worry. "Did Mama—"

Gavin pulled the boy to him and held him against his chest. For seven months he had known this hour was coming. Why then did it still catch him off guard, unprepared?

Gently, Shawn pushed himself away, as if to search an answer in his father's eyes.

"Our mom—" Gavin began, but the words would not come.

"What happened? Did she die?"

Couldn't there have been an easier, gentler way? he asked himself. *Wasn't there—*

"Did she, Dad?"

"It was time," he heard himself say. "It was finally time for her to go to Father in heaven."

Shawn stared at him for a moment. "You mean, she already went?"

Gavin nodded. "She wanted to stay—a little longer—but it was time." He pulled Shawn against him again and went on: "But she wasn't sad. We know our mom, don't we? She was looking forward to being with Heavenly Father again, just the same way she'll be looking forward to being with us again—someday."

"But I didn't want—" Shawn started to say.

Gavin pressed him close. *Hang on,* he kept telling himself. And for a moment neither of them spoke.

Finally he whispered in Shawn's ear: "She left you a message—to take good care of me." He felt Shawn's arms tighten around his neck. "And I told her—I promised her—you would."

"Oh, Daddy, I love you," he heard Shawn try to say before his voice broke and his body began to ripple in a series of quiet sobs.

For a long time they held to each other, and then once again, Shawn pulled back. "Her spirit—her spirit's with Heavenly Father then? Right now?"

Gavin nodded. "Right now." He hesitated. "Lucky, huh?"

Shawn nodded slightly, holding back the tears. "Yeah," he said huskily. "Yeah, lucky."

Shawn's head leaned forward against Gavin's shoulder, and Gavin rubbed smooth circles on the boy's back with the palm of his hand. After a while he whispered in his ear, "Why don't you come with me and sleep in my bed?"

Shawn didn't answer, but Gavin could feel him nestle closer against his chest. He picked him up and carried him from the room, stopping only to turn out the night lamp.

In his own bedroom, he tucked him under the blankets without turning on the light, then, still dressed, he slipped off his shoes and lay down beside him.

"Dad," he heard Shawn say, his voice somewhere between a whisper and a whimper. "Thanks for letting me be in here."

"It's okay," Gavin whispered back, pulling the boy an inch or two closer against him and realizing that he had done it as much for himself as for Shawn.

Two

More snow fell between the end of January and early April than he had ever remembered: it fell for days without stopping; it piled high against the porches, it hid mailboxes, it buried cars; new snow fell before the old snow had even begun to melt.

But April came in a welcome burst of blue skies and sunshine that transformed snowdrifts into puddles almost overnight. There was danger of sudden flooding and talk of sandbags, of diking, and even of possible evacuation. But most of all, there was a widespread feeling of relief that winter was over, an indescribable but undeniable joy that shone in people's faces and spread infectiously, uniting neighbors and strangers alike in a mysterious springtime bond.

And it was on one of those early April mornings, a Saturday, that he woke up suddenly remembering what Lois had made him promise about the book.

He had trouble finding it at first. He could almost picture it—on a shelf, in a box, in a drawer—but wherever he looked, it was never there. Finally, there it was: wedged between a box of old Christmas cards and a thin but glossy book of Victorian houses in San Francisco. It stood on a shelf in a closet he had not yet sorted. *Beautiful Stories from Shakespeare*, retold by E. Nesbit, published in 1907. On the brown cover, in black and rose and silver, was an illustration of Romeo and Juliet—and as in the many pen-and-ink drawings throughout the book, the familiar roles were played by children.

Memories of their Cleveland days flickered through his mind like an old-time movie on a pizza-parlor wall. The reason Lois had borrowed the book he had long forgotten; yet he remembered the embarrassment when Mrs. Kocherhans had continued to ask about it, claiming it had never been returned. He opened it up: dark-blue crayon marks swirled and zigzagged across the title page.

I was so embarrassed, he could hear Lois's voice lamenting—embarrassed not only that the book had not been returned after all, but also that Shawn had, in the meantime, decorated with a two-year-old's scrawl that opening page with its antique lettering and ornate border. *Please get it back to her for me . . .*

And he had promised. An unexpected sensation of pleasure mixed with a faint feeling of dread brushed by him like a ghost. He shivered, then puzzled over the sudden warmth that followed. He was prepared for the sense of dread: life was full of distasteful little chores that people keep shuffling to the back files of their minds to lose them or forget them. But what surprised him was the feeling of honest anticipation that seemed mingled with it.

Not that he looked forward to contacting Mrs. Kocherhans. Lois undoubtedly had known her better than he; it was only, in fact, as a plump, middle-aged figure with a sprinkling can or a flower pot that he could conjure up her image at all. She had simply been one of the inhabitants—well, maybe a little friendlier than most—

that you passed on the stairs or shared pleasantries with down at the mailboxes.

But then again, maybe there was more to it than that. There *had* been an applesauce cake involved. He remembered *that* because Lois had later asked for the recipe and had in fact several times made what became known in the house as "Mrs. Kocherhans's cake." And probably there had been more—things that a young wife and mother would share with or learn from the more experienced widow living alone next door. Maybe she wasn't even alive anymore. She certainly hadn't been old—but who could tell what might happen to a woman in her late fifties or early sixties living by herself. Or, for that matter, what might happen to a young mother of twenty-nine who less than a year ago had been making plans for many things that now would never come to pass. Mrs. Kocherhans herself might have passed on during those three years they had been gone. He didn't recall that they had even exchanged Christmas cards. Was it because of the lack of any truly lasting ties? Or out of embarrassment over the missing book?

But all that didn't matter now. Something he couldn't explain made him want to go back to those plain brick apartments on Grand Avenue. Just to clear the slate. Mailing the book, it occurred to him, wouldn't be quite enough. He wanted the experience of knocking on the door, of waiting to see if Mrs. Kocherhans—in her apron? or carrying a potted fern or geranium?—would answer the door. He wanted to tell her, in person, that Lois had died. Unless she had happened onto the obituary in the paper, she probably wouldn't know. Surely she would be touched. All the people in those apartments who had ever known Lois or even seen her in the laundry room or noticed her taking Shawn out for a walk in the stroller— surely they all would be touched. But he wouldn't try to find out if any of them were still there; the ones they had been closest to and kept in touch with had all moved, scattered among places like Detroit, Atlanta, and Sacramento.

But Mrs. Kocherhans should be told. Above all, she should have the book back. Standing in the bedroom with it in his hands now, he sniffed at the faint, musty pages and smiled at the child-duke disguised as a friar and encircled by an ornate frame of pale lavender. Understanding Lois's concern was not hard: a book like this, with or without the unsightly crayon marks, would be painful to lose. He glanced around the room. He had come to understand these kinds of things more and more.

"Shawn?" he asked, thinking he had heard someone stirring in the next room. He peeked into the boy's room at the rumpled but empty bed at the same time that he heard the faint growls, bumps, and screeches of Saturday-morning cartoons coming from the TV downstairs. From the top of the stairs he could see, by crouching, the pajama-clad figure huddled cross-legged in front of the garish colors that accompanied the roars and screeches of an animated adventure.

He had to call three times to get his attention. "Shawn! Do you want to go on a little trip?"

"Huh?" The boy looked around long enough to identify the location of the voice, but then turned back to the antics on the screen.

"After we get something to eat, I want to take you somewhere. Back where we lived when you were little."

"Okay," seemed to be the reply. But the boy only folded his arms and leaned in closer to the TV screen.

"Okay," Gavin mumbled, with a puzzled little shake of his head. "It may not be Pac-Man or the Smurfs," he went on talking to himself as he padded barefoot down the hall, "but it might be an adventure nonetheless."

* * * * *

He felt glad to be out on the road on such a clear, sunny day. There was something definitely exhilarating about speeding along in the open with the morning sun coming down through the windshield and the brisk fresh air, so long denied in favor of the stifling heater, now circulating through the open vents. He could smell the faint yet invigorating greenness of damp grasses, despite the fact that the fields, newly uncovered from months of snow, still wore shades of brown and yellow ochre. And the trees, even though leafless, seemed to be lightly tinged with an aura of fresh green.

"Feel like singing?" he asked suddenly, looking down at Shawn, who sat on the edge of the seat beside him, peering through the windshield.

"Like what?"

"Like—" he stalled. "Well, like, how about 'Raindrops Keep Fallin' on My Head'?"

But he knew even before Shawn cocked his head, squinted one eye, and scowled at him that he had made a bad choice. "*Raindrops*—are you kidding?"

"Well, I mean, the tune's right," he tried to defend himself. "Happy, bouncy—" He gave his head a little shake and shrugged. "Oh well, how about 'Popcorn Popping on the Apricot Tree'?"

He glanced over to see Shawn roll his eyes dramatically.

He gave in. "Okay, fella, *you* name it."

Shawn was quiet for a moment, staring straight ahead through the windshield. "I can't think of anything," he finally said.

"Well, we can't let a great day like this go to waste without a song! How about 'Down in the Valley'?"

Shawn shrugged. "Okay, I guess."

Gavin started out—"Down in the valley, the valley so

low"—and Shawn, still perched on the edge of the seat and staring out the windshield, joined in.

"The Old Gray Mare," "Daisy, Daisy," "Put on Your Old Gray Bonnet," "Take Me Out to the Ballgame," and several more they couldn't get all the way through followed.

"How do you know all those songs, anyway, Dad?" Shawn finally broke in. "Were they popular when you were little?"

Gavin had to think for a moment. "Not really. Some we sang in school, I guess, when I lived out in Utah. But I think I mainly got them from Grandma Terry. She used to rock and bounce me on her knee and sing all kinds of things— some without words even. Just 'doodlely, doodlely, diddlely dum' and stuff. She was Irish."

"Is that how they talk in Irishland—or Ireland—or whatever?"

"Ireland," Gavin answered. "No. It's just nonsense, I guess." He glanced over at Shawn. "Grandma would have had a great time with you. I wish you could have known her."

"But I *do* know her. I know Grandma Terry."

"I don't mean Grandma Terry in Florida. I mean *my* Grandma Terry—your great-grandmother."

"Did she live in Utah?"

"No, Boston. They came over from Ireland when she was a little girl. Then she met Grandpa Terry—*Great*-grandpa Terry—and they got married and moved to Nebraska."

"Where you were born—right?"

"Well—yes. But first, my dad was born there. Grandpa Terry. And then, about twenty-five years later, he married Grandma and I was born."

"Is Nebraska in Utah?"

"No. It's another state, quite far away, but not as far as

Ohio. We moved to Utah when I was seven. In fact, I can hardly remember Nebraska at all."

"Can you remember Utah?"

"Oh, sure. I can remember almost everything about Utah." An image flashed into his mind: red-rock cliffs rising up behind trees uncannily green, while white clouds overhead tumbled lazily in a sky of Kodachrome blue. "We lived there for ten whole years—all of my school days, in fact, except for the first year and the last." For a moment he saw himself catching minnows with a tin can and a wire strainer in a pond at the edge of town; then he was riding a bicycle, years later, down the same dusty road lined with cottonwoods.

"How come *I* never get to go to Utah?"

"You *have* been to Utah—once, anyway. I guess you wouldn't remember, though. You were only about two."

"Did you take me to see where you used to live?"

"No, not really. We just went through Salt Lake City on our way to San Francisco." He saw the brick house with the twin juniper trees where they had lived. Then the image shifted slightly to include him, big-eared and grinning, stiffly posed on the cement steps that led to the front door, and he realized that the picture in his head came to him as much from an old snapshot as from actual memory. The house stirred something in him. Why hadn't he ever gone back?

"Did Mama live there too?"

"Did Mama—" The question startled him back to the present moment, and he became aware again of the pale greens and yellow-browns of the Ohio countryside blurring past him on both sides. "You mean in Cedar City?"

"Cedar City or Utah or wherever it was that you—"

"Cedar City *is* Utah," he explained. "Way down in the southern part. But Mom never lived there. I didn't meet

Mom until after we left Utah and moved to the East. In fact, not until after I was in the army."

"You mean Mama was in the army too?" Shawn said, straightening up his back.

"No. I met her after I joined the Church—in Sunday School, in fact. In Fort Benning, Georgia."

"Mom told me about that," Shawn said with a faint smile. Then, seeming satisfied, he curled up on the seat and closed his eyes. Gavin glanced down in time to notice the boy's thumb drifting lazily up toward his mouth. But when Shawn's eyes opened and their gaze met, the thumb immediately disappeared somewhere beneath him. Then his eyes closed once more, and Gavin smiled to himself as they sped down the highway.

When they reached Cleveland it was already two-thirty in the afternoon. The sun was still shining brightly, the sky clear as ever, and the suburbs alive with children on tricycles and mothers pushing strollers. Yet he felt the first tinge of hesitation as he turned a corner and started down a street that began to bring back memories. Was it that a certain tangle of memories—mostly fond but all connected to Lois—was about to be stirred to the surface? Or, he wondered, was it simply the awkwardness of returning something after such a long time and having to apologize for the damage? Yet, for all the uneasiness that shivered through him, the tingle of exhilaration still lingered. It felt good, he reassured himself, just to clear the slate.

"Is this where we lived?" Shawn asked, scooting himself to the very edge of the seat and holding onto the dashboard.

"More or less. Does anything look familiar?"

"Uh-uh. Well, maybe a little, I guess."

"You were pretty young."

"But I do remember my little red wagon."

"Really? Or is it just the snapshot you remember?"

"No, my *wagon!* I do, really. It had a picture of a teddy bear on each side and some writing." He sat still for a moment as though thinking, then blurted out, "But how come we sold it?"

"It was really teeny, remember? I think some neighbors offered us a couple of dollars for it. Besides, you can't hold on to everything, can you?"

"Yes, you can," he mumbled sullenly. "If you really want to."

Gavin sighed. "I wish it were that easy."

Shawn looked intently out the windshield, sometimes whipping his head around to stare out the side window as they passed something. "Do you think we can find who's got my red wagon?"

"I doubt it," Gavin smiled. "Besides, it wouldn't be yours anymore, would it?"

"Uh-*huh*," Shawn nodded emphatically.

"What would you do with it if we found it?"

"Just look at it," Shawn answered.

Gavin turned a corner. The trees were bigger, houses had been repainted, a corner building torn down. He began looking for familiar markers and the sign that would say Grand Avenue.

"Wouldn't you like to go back to Cedar City and look for some of *your* stuff?" Shawn suddenly asked.

"Uh-uh," he answered teasingly. But it struck him as strange that his answer made him feel a slight tinge of guilt. There really wasn't anything of his left in Cedar City; when they had moved there from Nebraska, they had brought everything with them; and then when they had finally left there for Pennsylvania ten years later, they had taken everything away. The house, maybe—*that* he might be interested in seeing, but there wouldn't be anything else left from those days. Unless, perhaps, some of the people . . .

Suddenly there it was, black letters on the thin rectangle of white: Grand Avenue. He turned sharply to the right, then strained to take in each detail as they passed slowly down the street. Things seemed slightly changed; yet somehow all remained almost exactly the way he remembered it. The brick apartment house was on the right at the end of the block. *Oh, Lois,* something in him wanted to cry. *Why aren't you here with us?* Why, he wanted to know, weren't they all still up there sitting around the dinette set, Shawn spreading cereal on the tray of the highchair they had bought at Goodwill, Lois laughing in the way she used to, tipping her head forward and then throwing it back.

"Is this it? Is it?" Shawn was asking as they slowed down.

"Do you recognize it?"

"Well, sort of." But Shawn's eyes still waited for a confirmation.

"You guessed it," Gavin told him. "But tell me this, Mr. Memory Box: which apartment did we live in?" He was glad Shawn was here with him; the chitter-chatter helped to ease the pain that was trying to break loose inside.

"Which one?" he asked again, turning off the key and leaning forward to look from the car at the building ahead of them, his eyes moving upward to the window on the third floor where the yellow dinette set had been.

Shawn hesitated a moment, then looked at him. "That one?"

"Which one?"

"The one where the blue curtains are? Or how about that one next to it?"

"Nope. Neither of those. It was—"

"Wait! Was it upstairs? It was upstairs, wasn't it? I think I can remember lots of steps or something."

"*Lots* of steps. About four flights," Gavin helped him. "In fact, look up there at that window next to the one with the bird cage. See it?" He pointed with one hand while his other slipped around the boy's shoulder and helped tilt his chin to look up to the third floor.

"See it?"

"Yeah," Shawn breathed excitedly. "Can we go in it?"

"Not really," he answered, feeling a vestige of regret mingled with relief. "But we'll visit the lady next door, Mrs. Kocherhans, if she still lives there."

They climbed from the car and walked across the grass to the apartment building, Gavin carrying the Shakespeare book in one hand and holding onto Shawn with the other. Together they climbed the zigzagging flight of stairs that led to the third floor. For a moment they stood hand in hand at the top of the landing, silently facing the door where they had once lived. But then Gavin gave Shawn's hand a little squeeze, and they turned and rang the bell at the door marked N. Kocherhans.

It took her a few minutes to answer.

"Yes?" she said, glancing down at Shawn then up at Gavin. Even without a potted plant or a sprinkling can, she looked surprisingly the same. But he saw in an instant that she had not recognized him.

"Mrs. Kocherhans, do you remember—"

Then it clicked. "My goodness," she began, and her face broke into a smile while her hands wiped themselves instantly on her apron and then reached out to clasp his.

"Of course I remember, of course! Come in!"

"Gavin Terry," he felt obliged to help out in case she had forgotten. "And this is Shawn, remember?"

She reached down and placed her hands on each side

of his face. "Oh, my goodness, yes. Of course I remember. But what a little man you've become!"

He knew it was coming next, and it did: "And where's your wife—uh—what's her name? Lois, yes?"

"Lois—" he began, "Lois passed away a couple of months ago."

He dreaded the look on people's faces that inevitably followed. Mrs. Kocherhans's fingers slipped up to her chin and along her cheek. "No," she breathed. "Oh, no." Then, "How? What happened?"

"Cancer," he said. "It took us all by surprise. Although we *did* know," he added hastily, "for several months, in fact."

"And when did this happen?" Mrs. Kocherhans asked, feeling behind her for a chair and dropping quietly into it as she motioned for them to sit down.

"In January." He felt Shawn pressing in close against him, and he sat down on the couch, pulling the boy in beside him.

"Oh, my," he heard her mutter half under her breath.

To fill an awkward pause, he found himself rushing ahead to the matter of the book. "One of the reasons I'm here," he began, "is that—she—she had found this book." He held it out to her. "Remember?"

"My book," she whispered.

"She was sure she had returned it. Remember how we looked for it?"

Mrs. Kocherhans reached out and gently took the book. "Oh, my—the poor dear."

"One of the last things she asked me was to return it. She found it among our things after all and was insistent that you get it back."

Mrs. Kocherhans smoothed her hand over the sepia-embossed cover.

"I'm afraid that—" he began. "I'm afraid there are

some marks—on the front page, I think—that Shawn must have made with a crayon."

She opened the book without saying a word, but he could see she was trying to smile.

"If there were a way I could replace it," he hurried on, "I—"

"Oh, please, Mr. Terry," she said, holding out a hand as if to stop him. "Please, such marks, such a little thing as that—" Suddenly she directed her gaze toward Shawn and her eyes grew genuinely warm. "You wanted to make some fancy designs, didn't you?"

"We apologize," Gavin said as kindly as he could. "We're sorry to have kept this for so long."

"Please," she said again, raising her palm. "It's enough simply that you found it and went out of your way to bring it back." She rubbed her hand across the cover and then opened one or two of the pages. "And I thought it was lost forever." She suddenly looked up at Gavin. "Where is it you're coming from? You still live in Cleveland?"

"No. I finished school that last year here. Then I was offered a job with Stanhauser and Company in Columbus. I'm a statistician," he added.

"Ah, yes," she said. Then she made a little clicking noise with her tongue and shook her head. "Such a long way, and just to return a book. But what a surprise, and how grateful I am to have it again! Bless your heart—and your dear sweet wife . . ."

They stayed for half an hour more while she showed them photographs from a shoe box, fed them chocolate-chip ice cream, and reminisced about other Aprils, other Novembers. By three-thirty they had told her good-bye and watched her wave from the third-story window as they drove away.

He felt glad they had come. And the feeling, a sense of relief, of liberation even, stayed with him throughout the afternoon as they rode around the town, ate hamburgers and malts at a drive-in, then sat through one-and-a-half showings of *The Black Stallion*. It was with him still when they checked in at the Whitlock Motel and lay side by side in the big bed with the chenille spread.

Inside his head the wheels were turning. He could almost feel them shifting and revolving as he tipped his head back on the pillow and stared at the ceiling.

"—be fun if we could stay in a different motel every night for a whole year," Shawn was saying.

"Yeah," he sighed in agreement. A thought occurred to him, then took definite shape. "Maybe I couldn't promise a whole year, but would you settle for two or three weeks?"

He felt Shawn turn abruptly to look at him. "Really?"

"Really," he answered, still looking at the ceiling and listening to the whisper-like rotation of the wheels in his head. Finally he turned to face Shawn, whose brown eyes were only inches away, "How would it be if we took a trip out to Utah—to Cedar City?"

"Really?" Shawn repeated. "Could we really?"

He shrugged his shoulders. "Why not? I've got at least twenty days of vacation coming up in June. We could take four or five days to get there and then—"

Shawn raised himself up on one elbow and stared at him. "Are you kidding?"

"I'm serious," he found himself saying. Like slides in a slide show, images of Cedar City faded in and out before him. A face or two, not thought of in years, came into focus, then blurred into something else.

"But how come? Just to see it?"

"More or less," he said quietly. But most of all, he thought, to settle a few old scores. *To clear the slate.* "There are some things, two or three things, that I'd like to straighten out." He hoped Shawn wouldn't ask what they were because he was not yet sure he even knew. He saw the face of J. D. Sargent—blond, blue-eyed, and freshly scrubbed—rising up onto the screen of his mind, but what seemed to be a slight touch of resentment in his smile made Gavin blink the image away. The next image was better: Mr. Shipley, bulging and bald, leaning over his desk in the English room. Making amends there wouldn't be so hard . . .

"Are you sure?" Shawn was saying. He was sitting up now.

"I think so," he said, and he raised himself to a sitting position. It was impossible to think of everything right now, and he was not entirely sure he wanted to, but there would be time for that. In any case—he felt the shiver of exhilaration again—it would be worth it: to clear the slate. Delivering the lost book had triggered something in him he hadn't counted on; but whatever it was, it excited him now. He longed for the chance to clear up, once and for all, the old memories, to exorcise the old ghosts, to do a thorough house cleaning. And there really wasn't much, was there? The exam, J. D., the election, maybe Bryce Gunderson . . .

"Oh, Dad, let's really do it!" Shawn urged.

"We'll do it," he said, feeling something in his chest he hadn't felt for years. It was like being back on the track, body stretched tautly in the extended crouch that kept you close to the starting line yet ready to spring foward at the explosion of the gun, the hair standing up on the back of your neck, your heart pounding with a painfully thrilling mixture of anticipation and dread—

"Great!" Shawn yelled, his voice like a gunshot.

Three

In Indiana they sang "In the Good Old Summertime"; crossing Illinois they perfected "Michael, Row the Boat Ashore" and "Tom Dooley"; throughout Iowa they memorized the verse and chorus of "Oh, What a Beautiful Morning"; and "There's a Long, Long Trail A-Winding" helped them to get through most of Nebraska. By Wyoming they had added "Where Has My Little Dog Gone," "My Bonnie," and "Little Tom Tinker" to their repertoire and revived "Take Me Out to the Ball Game" and "Down in the Valley."

Too hoarse to sing at the top of his lungs anymore and frustrated that he could remember only two or three lines from any one of a number of songs that came to his mind, Gavin sat back and let Shawn teach him Primary songs as they made their way across Utah.

"How about 'Book of Mormon Stories'? Do you know that one?" Shawn asked brightly.

"Mmmm, not really," Gavin answered. "You have to remember I didn't ever go to Primary."

"How come? Were you naughty or something?"

"Naughty?" Gavin laughed. "Of course not. I was perfect. Actually, I was probably a brat, but that's not the point. I didn't even know about Primary back then because I wasn't a Mormon. Remember? Not until after I joined the army."

"Oh, yeah," Shawn said. "But you should have gone *then*."

"In the army? Are you kidding?"

"Well, just to learn the songs, I mean."

Gavin laughed. "Well, guess I goofed. Now you'll have to teach me."

"You always bumble up the words, though."

"Hey, nice talk about your old dad, calling him a bumble," Gavin teased.

Shawn blushed. "Well, sometimes you are. I mean, you always forget that part in 'Give, Said the Little Stream' about 'I'm small I know, but wherever I go—'"

"Try me. I'm a whiz."

So "Give, Said the Little Stream" got them almost to Vernal.

By the time they reached the stretch of prairie, hills, and sagebrush between Fillmore and Parowan, Gavin began to feel that his mental list was beginning to take some final shape. He realized that some long-forgotten incident might still come wiggling its way up through the debris of the past, yet he felt quite confident that the long expanses of Iowa, Nebraska, and Wyoming had given him sufficient time to dig around in memory's detritus, to sift **and sort** through odd scraps and tatters of recollections, so **that** the cluster of reminiscences he had dusted off and **selected** really were, perhaps, the most significant, the most hauntingly persistent.

He had tried to assign them an order, not a ranking according to importance exactly, but one based more on how easily they might be dealt with. Looking up Mr. Shipley, surely still as permanent a fixture at the high school as he had ever been, shouldn't be too difficult, unless, by some chance, he had suddenly died. How old would he be now after thirteen years? Sixty? Sixty-five? Retired already? It was hard to imagine.

And then Mrs. Mendenhall. A bit of uneasiness there. What did he expect to do? Ask if he and Shawn could go into the backyard and finish a job left undone for fifteen or sixteen years? Maybe the whole thing was ludicrous. Best, perhaps, just to give her back three or four dollars. And then again, maybe she wouldn't even be there anymore. He imagined the house boarded up or even torn down. She had been an old, white-haired widow even back in the mid-sixties. What chance was there that she could still be puttering around the lilac bushes and plum trees today? He had goofed that one. Probably no way to make amends now. Why hadn't he simply sent her a check for four dollars long ago? He felt irritated, disappointed in himself. Too bad about that one. He just might have waited too long.

Maybe Bryce Gunderson next. But that certainly would not be one of the easy ones. Maybe it should be last on the list. Or maybe—no, it had to be on the list somewhere. But it was in a different category, a kind of class by itself. With J. D. Sargent, it would be easier, infinitely easier, because he had consciously or unconsciously felt he should do it for a long time. But Bryce Gunderson was another matter, and he found himself mentally dragging his feet even now. With J. D. he could honestly say that there were no hard feelings, not on his part at least. Time seemed to have really erased any kind of pride or embarrassment there. But Bryce? What was it? Just an honest-to-goodness dislike that had never dissipated or mellowed?

With J. D. it should be different. Because they had once

been so close, there was a good chance that he could still close the gap that had grown between them, maybe even erase some of the old pain. Maybe—

But even finding J. D. could be a bigger problem than he was prepared for since he seemed like the type that would not have stayed around Cedar City. He would probably have gone away to some university or another. He found himself wondering what field J. D. would have chosen to study and whom he would have married. He could, in fact, have married Sharilyn Tebbs right out of high school. Sharilyn Tebbs as a thirty-year-old woman was hard to imagine. The only way he could picture her now was in the short, white pleated skirt and matching sneakers, two massive pompons making a red-and-gold blur around her as she shook and shimmied and kicked her tanned legs high into the air.

If only he had kept in touch some way. Even a Christmas card—or a postcard from time to time—would have helped. Someone had sent a card to him, hadn't she? Someone had found his address—Sharilyn? Vickie? the Sorenson girl? There had been a card of some sort; he was sure of that. But he had never answered, and after that there had never been anything else.

His parents had kept in touch with someone. The Bigelows? Someone without children his age, at any rate. He could remember scouring the back of a Christmas card one year for any scrap of news about anyone he knew. It couldn't have been that he just hadn't cared; he could remember wondering about different people from time to time and feeling sure that, one day, he would be suddenly brought up to date on all that had taken place.

But it hadn't ever happened. Probably his own fault, he realized. He hardly wrote letters now, and he certainly had not been any better at seventeen. And then the election had soured everything for a while. Even now, a little, he had to admit. But he couldn't let those feelings drag on anymore. It was time to bury all of that, once and for all.

"So," he said aloud. "It's done. Over. Gone."

"What is?" Shawn asked, sitting up.

"I thought you were asleep." He glanced down at Shawn who yawned and then curled up again on the seat beside him.

"I was—sort of," came the answer, followed by an audible yawn. "Are we almost there?"

"Not long now. We've just passed through Parowan, so we're close." What if J. D. were living in Parowan, he wondered. Not likely. But then, he could be anywhere: Salt Lake City, Provo, Ogden, maybe Denver, L. A.—even Cleveland or Columbus! The thought struck him as both amusing and unsettling. What if the people he needed to see were all ironically scattered throughout the East somewhere. Was it possible that he might actually be unable to contact any of the people on his list? Thirteen years *was* thirteen years, after all.

And yet, just driving down the highway seemed to be closing the gap the years had made. A damp, grassy smell from a field, the red-orange appearing in an occasional hill—they somehow shriveled the years and made him feel, for the first time, that maybe he had not been away as long as he'd thought.

Had he remembered everything? He started to make another mental check of the list, but his mind snagged on an image and he was forced to linger there awhile.

It was a dance at the high school: crepe-paper streamers drooped overhead, and somewhere in the dimness of the gym a band played "This Guy's in Love with You." For some reason, he couldn't quite bring back the face of the girl he was dancing with, but through the crowd he could see Sharilyn in a pale blue dress glancing back at him over her shoulder.

He winced a little. Who had she been with? Not J. D. And not Bryce. That had been some consolation at least. He remembered thinking, and not without at least a tinge of resentment, that when Sharilyn hadn't asked him, he had been sure she must have asked Bryce. He could still remember the days leading up to the dance. What did they call it then? Girls' Day Dance? Or something more? Preference—that was it. A dressy affair, he remembered. The girls had even bought carnation boutonnieres for the guys. But he could remember trying to act aloof—

So, do you think Sharilyn's going to ask you? He could almost hear J. D.'s voice.

I doubt it, he had probably lied.

Of course she'll ask you. Why wouldn't she?

Maybe she'll ask you.

That'll be the day. You know who she's probably really going to ask?

Maybe the words weren't quite right, but he could still remember the feeling: how could J. D. say *Of course she'll ask you* and then, in almost the same breath, come back with *You know who she's probably really going to ask?* But that was like J. D.

Bryce, they had both agreed. *She'll probably ask Big Bryce Gunderson.* But they had both been wrong. Who had it been anyway? Some out-of-towner. A lanky basketball player from St. George or somewhere that he had never seen before. But J. D. had known him, or at least known who he was.

Sharilyn, reaching up during that slow tune to put her arm around her gangly partner yet casting a glance back over her shoulder . . . Why did an image like that keep floating back out of nowhere after all these years? Something about that dance made him ache even now. But it wasn't Sharilyn. At least not now. How trivial it all seemed: pompons at a football game, a backward glance at a preference ball—who cares? But the ironical truth was there, it occurred to him: the images we would choose to remember are not always the ones that choose to haunt us.

He watched the landscape speeding toward him. Somewhere, beyond those low hills ahead, would be Cedar City. He found himself almost pronouncing the words aloud: Cedar City . . . But would it even look the same?

Another image: Vickie Simpkins and two or three other girls in a Chevy dragging Main Street on a warm spring evening. A honk of the horn. Two minutes later, a U-turn, and the car coming back up the street, Vickie leaning out the window and yelling something to him. Back up Main Street, then down again. Another honk of the horn, another U-turn, and this time the girls in the faded Chevrolet pulling up in front of the Cedar movie theater.

Are you really moving away? There must have been things said before that, but whatever they were he had long forgotten.

Yeah, why?

Scout's honor?

Scout's honor. Why?

I just wondered. Pause. *I heard you weren't.*

Well, if I win the election—

I heard you weren't moving anyway. Vickie's eyes, testing him.

Who said that? Of course we're moving. My dad's been transferred—to Pennsylvania. But I might stay. And I'll stay for sure if I win the election.

Stay with who?

Shrug. *Somewhere. Don't worry, if I'm student-body president, I'll stay.* If someone had told him six months earlier that they were going to be transferred, he was sure that J. D. would have offered to have him stay, perhaps even begged for him to stay with his family to finish his senior year. Especially if there had been any thought that he might run for student-body president. But the nominations and primary election had changed all that. Who would have ever suspected that it would be J. D. he would be running against in the finals?

Anyway, who said we weren't moving?

Somebody.

Who was it?

It's just that I heard J. D. telling some guys that—

J. D.?

Vickie's eyes glancing away and then back again. *Well, it's just that I heard him saying something about how you didn't really have to move—that it was just a way to get sympathy votes . . .*

Whatever he had answered he couldn't remember, but her words had cut him; even now he could feel the wound. Had J. D. deliberately started that lie in order to swing the election in his own favor?

"Is that it?" Shawn was sitting forward on the edge of the seat now.

Gavin tried to push the memory from his mind, but images of Vickie and J. D. faded in and out of his thoughts. "Yeah," he answered, almost absentmindedly. "That's it."

A green exit sign loomed ahead beside the highway.

Whose idea had it been to tell people that, if he won the election, he could stay on and finish high school there, but if he lost, he'd have to move to Pennsylvania? Someone in his campaign party? It wasn't a lie, and it wasn't something dreamed up just to win votes. It had been a fact.

But who would you stay with? His dad's voice echoed over the years.

I don't know—Sargents maybe. There's lots of possibilities. Just as long as I can finish my senior year here and not have to—

It could be pretty miserable, remember, staying at J. D.'s if you won and he lost.

And what if J. D. wins? his mother had put in.

Yes, what about that? his father echoed.

I guess I could ask Clea Bigelow about the possibility of room and board, his mother tried to help. *Their kids are all raised and gone now and—*

But there had been no need.

His mind flashed to election night, to the dance at the high school and the crowd of students and parents lining the gym when the results were announced. *Try to look happy,* he had told himself when J. D.'s name was read over the loudspeaker. *Applaud and support him.* But the muscles in his face felt foreign and his eyes smarted. And he remembered knowing then, with certainty, that he would move to Pennsylvania with his parents.

He slowed down for the off-ramp and circled back around under the freeway, heading east into town. Shawn inched forward on the seat, almost standing now, and turned to grin at his father.

"This is Cedar City," he said softly.

Gavin slowed down, peering intently at one side of the road, then the other. He wanted something to hang onto, something that would snag at him and say, "Remember me?" But it was all strangely familiar yet unfamiliar at the same time.

He turned left almost automatically and made his way past the college campus, greener and shadier than he remembered it. Then, beyond the school, another left and a right. Passing the house with all the flowers almost made him dizzy with the remembered perfume of sweet peas. Some houses had changed color; others seemed to have added a porch or a carport. All seemed smaller than remembered, yet the cottonwoods and blue spruce loomed larger than ever.

"See that house?" he whispered to Shawn. "The one with those pointed juniper trees?"

"You mean those kind of Christmasy trees in front?"

"That's it. That's where I lived."

"Oh, Dad, let's go in—can we? Park, please, and let's go in. Maybe we'll find some of your old toys."

Gavin eased the car to a stop between the stuccoed house that used to be the Bentleys' and the brick one where he had lived. For a moment he sat looking through the windshield, almost waiting to see himself pedaling down the street on his bicycle. It was hard to imagine that all the neighborhood kids would have grown up and probably moved away, that people would have married, found jobs elsewhere, even died. A balding man in his late thirties or forties was mowing the lawn in front of the house across the street, but nothing about him looked familiar.

"Can we, Dad?"

He found himself nodding slowly, but his mind ran on, asking questions he couldn't answer.

Four

By six-thirty that evening they had checked in at a
motel with a pool, found pizza at a new little place where
no one looked familiar, and driven two or three times
down his old street, finally stopping near the house where
the lawnmower now rested in the driveway and only a
sweet, moist, grassy smell lingered on the quiet lawn. A
little girl, about ten, played hopscotch by herself on the
sidewalk.

"What do you say we take a little walk?" Gavin asked
Shawn. The boy smiled and shrugged. They got out,
stretched; then Gavin led the way to where the girl hopped
on one foot, her sandy curls bobbling, as she made her
way through the crude, chalk-drawn rectangles.

"Hi," Gavin started. The girl looked back, mumbled
"Hi" in return, then gave two or three awkward hops and
spun around to stare at them.

"Do you live here?" he asked, pointing to the house
with the newly mown lawn.

"Uh-uh," she answered. "I live *there.*" She pointed back
behind her.

"What's your name?" he asked.

"Mindy," she answered. "Mindy Bettinson."

The name meant nothing. "Didn't—didn't Winegars used to live here?"

The girl shrugged. "Frandsens live there now."

Another unfamiliar name. "And there?"

"Haroldsons."

Familiar. No faces came to mind, but the name seemed right. "How about across the street?" He pointed to his old house.

"Rinderhagens." She looked at him. "Who are you looking for?"

"Nobody really. It's just that—I used to live here a long time ago. Over there."

"We wanted to look inside," Shawn bravely volunteered, as if she were the one in charge.

"We rang the bell earlier," Gavin explained, "but—"

"Rinderhagens are still on vacation. But they're coming back next Saturday."

Maybe she *was* the one in charge. He was amazed at how much she seemed to know, how little he remembered. He decided to try a name on her: "Do you know anyone in Cedar City named J. D. Sargent? James DeLyle Sargent?" It wasn't impossible, it occurred to him, that he was even mayor of Cedar City.

She shook her head.

He looked up and down the street. He could try the Haroldsons; but he wished he could remember for sure who they were. Better still, if he could just spend a few minutes with a phone book—

A blue pickup coming down the street slowed to a stop a few feet in front of them. A man in boots and cowboy hat hopped out and hurried across the sidewalk. "Howdy do, Mindy Lou," he said, tipping his hat to the girl.

Gavin gave a little start. Although the name was slow

in coming, he knew that this was someone he had known. His mind raced to grasp onto a name or a family he could link with the big, sun-tanned cowboy, but he felt a certain satisfaction nonetheless that at least he had found his first truly familiar face.

"Remember me?" he found himself asking. "Gavin Terry. We used to live here back in the sixties."

"Why, sure I do—I think. Didn't your dad used to be county agent? Or run that experiment farm?"

Gavin hesitated. "No, not *my* dad. He was supervisor for the forest service."

The cowboy pushed his hat back and wiped his forehead with the back of his hand. "Well, I think I remember. You do look familiar, I'll say that. How's it been goin', anyway?"

Gavin found himself shrugging. He still didn't remember for sure who the man was, but now it didn't seem quite as important. "Things are okay, I guess," he mumbled. But then he found a question burgeoning inside him: "I was wondering if—uh—J. D. Sargent was still around anywhere."

"J. D. Sargent? You mean Millie and DeLyle's boy? Believe he's down there in St. George, ain't he?"

"I don't know. I've been gone for a—"

"Yeah, I'm pretty sure he's in real estate or somethin' or other down there in St. George."

"How about—"

"Hey, I've gotta get goin'—but it's sure good seein' ya again." He turned back to the girl on the sidewalk. "Hey, Mindy Lou, go tell your grandpa I've come for that saddle and hackamore of his." She turned and hurried back toward her house, and the cowboy, repeating once again "Good to see ya" as he stuck out a big, rough, and rusty hand, strode off behind her.

"Dad," Shawn was saying while he tugged at Gavin's hand. "Dad, was that a real cowboy?"

"It was, actually. About as real as you're going to find these days, I guess."

"And you knew him?"

"Not really."

For the next hour they strolled through the evening calm while the last rays of the sun filtered warmly through the trees. They were able to find the Haroldsons, who remembered him; they chattered for a few minutes with a young schoolteacher from Nevada who wasn't familiar with most of the names Gavin mentioned; and for a brief moment they exchanged pleasantries with an old Mrs. Smoot whom he'd almost forgotten.

It was still light when they drove by the corner where he had remembered the little frame grocery store, and a wave of nostalgia swept through him when he found it still there. The giant Coca-Cola advertisement had been painted over, but a sign across the front still proclaimed it HANSENS' GROCERY. It was closed, though, a little homemade sign on the glass door announcing OPEN FROM 8:00 A.M. TO 8:00 P.M. He looked at his watch— seventeen minutes past eight—and drove slowly away, fighting off a faint feeling of disappointment.

And maybe it was an attempt to compensate for that feeling that made him slow down as he turned the next corner and found himself driving by the blue-brick house with the dark porch that he remembered as Bryce Gunderson's.

"Are we going to visit somebody?" Shawn asked.

"Maybe," he said, turning off the key and looking back at the house. It was strange, ironic even, that he was parked here in front of Gunderson's. He tried to picture the order of things on the list that had gone through his mind so often during the long trip west, but the list had fallen apart and disintegrated in his mind. Seeing Bryce Gunderson had not been at the top of the list; in fact, he realized now, it might possibly have been the only item that he could actually say he dreaded.

Once more he cast a glance back over his shoulder at the bluish-gray brick house with the shadowy porch. He had never been inside it that he could remember. But what reason would he have had, anyway? Had he ever liked Bryce Gunderson?

A hazy image skittered across his mind: a vacant lot, a gloomy afternoon, and three boys—none of them more than eleven but all of them seeming to tower above him.

"Get out of here!" the biggest, named Bryce, snarled.

"I don't have to," he remembered saying weakly.

"You don't *what?*" Bryce retorted, his fierce eyes narrowing.

And perhaps he had mumbled back, once more, his feeble defiance.

"You stupid little runt! Get out of here before we sic our dog on ya!"

What had he done? Inched forward? Probably not. Refused to budge? Possibly—though he still remembered clearly the fear quivering through his body.

"Get 'im!"

He had run then. He remembered the big, brown, hairless dog leaping at him, almost knocking him down, and he remembered it coming back again, growling, snarling, tearing with its teeth at his hip. He remembered holding his side and crying as he ran, limping, for the remaining two or three blocks home. He remembered the fierce sting of iodine and his mother incredulously asking, "You mean they *made* the dog bite you?"

He got out of the car, trying not to think about it, and then lifted Shawn out and onto the sidewalk. A small irrigation ditch, almost covered with long grass, ran between the sidewalk and the road. Shawn squatted down and dropped broken sticks into the gurgling water.

"Can I just play here?"

Gavin hesitated. "For a moment. Maybe nobody's even home. Let me check."

The sun was down now, and the first lavender-gray of evening had fallen over the quiet neighborhood. A horse whinnied somewhere, and from far off came the faint sound of someone practicing the piano. He opened the wire gate and went up the walk to the big porch. Although it was just getting dusk, he had the feeling that, if someone were home, lights would probably already be on inside.

He stood on the porch for a moment, then rang the bell. Once or twice during the trip from Ohio he had tried to rehearse some things he might say. But waiting in front of the screen door, he could feel the words abandoning him, and his heart seemed to beat too loud, too fast, for him to even think. *Maybe*, he thought, *I have never forgiven him. Maybe I'm not ready, even yet, for this.* The bullying threats in the vacant lot, the terrifying attack of the big ugly dog—this was forgiven. They had been young, foolish, showing off strength, experimenting with power. But the other—

He rang the bell again.

What about the other? Again, an image skirted along the edge of his mind.

They were standing by the big rocks in front of the school on a late fall evening, he and J. D. Fifteen or sixteen years old now, they had just combed their hair and cinched in their wide belts on their flared-bottom denims. They reeked of bay rum or Mennen's Skin Bracer, their chins still smarting from the first proud but inexperienced encounters with the razor. He imagined them now, assuming casual poses there in the crisp night air, waiting for the girls and their pompons to burst through the double doors.

Then abruptly a car pulled up and Bryce Gunderson—hadn't he been the first in the class to drive?—bounded up onto the steps, thrusting out his chest and his jaw as he blurted out, "I'm warning you, Terry. If I see you hanging around Sharilyn Tebbs one more time, I'm going to smash your stupid face in."

He took a deep breath and rang the bell one more time, shifting weight uneasily as though feeling a chill. But it occurred to him that the evening was actually warm and that the coolness making him shiver was left over from that November evening fifteen or sixteen years ago.

"I mean it, Terry," Bryce was snarling. "Don't you let me catch you hanging around her—ever! At school or anyplace else—okay?"

"I don't even know what you're talking about," he had managed to say, reaching his hands up to loosen Bryce's grip on his shirt collar.

"Well, you better find out fast, because I don't like you, Terry." Then Bryce had shoved him so unexpectedly that he had almost fallen back against the rocks.

How often he had played back that scene in his mind. Sometimes, in replays, he had pulled back his fist and shot out a blow that sent Bryce reeling, in slow motion, onto the sidewalk. Sometimes J. D. had stepped in and helped him push Bryce away. Still other times he had simply straightened up his shoulders and delivered a comment—something so brilliant and literate and appropriately cutting that it had caused his aggressor to shrivel and cower until he finally sank back into the dark and chilly night. But despite the heroics of the manufactured replays, the humiliating reality of the actual event always rose up to haunt him.

He rang the bell a third time, knowing now that no one would answer. Again, a tinge of disappointment: why couldn't he, once and for all, unburden himself of the old anger, get rid of all the old hatred? But a feeling of relief was there as well: for how do you ask someone to forgive you for all the years you've never liked them? Was he really prepared now, even though he honestly yearned for the release, to make a total turnabout in his feelings?

He looked out into the oncoming twilight where Shawn scurried along the ditch bank, anxiously watching the plight of some stick boat. His heart ached for his own lost innocence, for a time when summer seemed as if it would last forever and the only worry in the world was the momentary anxiety that a popsicle-stick canoe might catch in the tall grasses or get lodged somewhere where the water ran under the road.

Shawn had crossed the street now and squatted at the spot where the little irrigation ditch reappeared from under the asphalt on the other side of the road. Then, in a split second, the parallel struck him: J. D., Sharilyn, Bryce, all the others—for ten years he had watched them all bumbling down life's river until they had all disappeared under some bridge, and now, thirteen years later, here he was like Shawn, waiting anxiously to see how they would come out on the other side.

He took one glance back at the darkened house, felt a last tug of relief and regret, and stepped off the porch and started down the sidewalk. But just as he reached the gate, a voice from somewhere made him stop. He looked off toward the wooden fence that ran along one side of the lot and saw, in the waning light, a young woman with pale hair standing on the other side.

"There's nobody home," he thought he heard her call.

He hesitated a moment. Then, as if something drew him, he found himself walking across the lawn to where she stood facing him from the other side of the fence. She seemed strangely out of place: something about the paleness of her face and her hair, and the way she wore it long yet fastened somehow at the back, made her look foreign—Slavic or Scandinavian. And the Old-World look of a country peasant girl increased even more as he drew closer, for he saw that she held in her arms a bunch of long-stemmed flowers, a smudge of dark soil on the inside of her arm apparently left from having just cut them.

"They're gone," he heard her say, and his eyes drifted back to her face. A faint shock shivered through him as he saw something in her pale blue eyes that seemed to come rocketing back through the years, piercing painfully through him, then lodging itself there, like heavy lead, inside.

"Don't I—" he began, feeling the hair rising on the back of his neck.

"You're Gavin Terry, aren't you?" she asked.

He studied her face—the pale eyes, the faint pink in her cheeks, the way her chin had a slight dip in it. He felt just on the verge of placing her, but the mixture of familiar and unfamiliar continued to make his head swim. He felt again the twinge of pain from something sharp, cold, and heavy inside.

She turned her head away slightly, as if uncomfortable, and for a second he caught a glimpse of who she had been, years before. Again, the spasm of pain.

They were at a dance. Crepe-paper streamers, pinkish-gold lights, the melancholy lament of a saxophone. But she was not there. Sharilyn was there—not with him, nor J. D., nor even Bryce, but with the gangly basketball player from St. George. And whoever he held—Vickie? Carol Ann Snow? the Sorensen girl?—somehow was not important. What did matter was that Sharilyn was with someone else. And also something more.

"You wouldn't remember me," the woman across the fence was saying. "I was a year younger—"

"Oh, but I do," he cut in, his mind still groping for the name that wouldn't come.

"Zin Stokes. I'm sure you wouldn't remember."

"No," he swallowed, "I do!" Zinnie Stokes. Zinnia Stokes. No one in the world had a name like that. Not in real life anyway. The Negro mammy in a movie or some spindly black woman from a Southern short story maybe, but not in real life. *Zinnie, Zinnie, tall and skinny . . .* She might have been thin—thin and pale with hair the color of bleached corn husks—but never very tall surely. But then not very pretty either—

"Who—who were you looking for?" she asked, seeming a little nervous now.

Again he found himself studying her face. Maybe it was a trick played by the dimming daylight, maybe an illusion caused by the faint rosy glow left in the darkening sky behind him that gave her skin a clear, healthy glow and made her blonde hair shine, but he felt overwhelmed by something indescribably lovely in her face, so incredibly different from the Zinnia Stokes he had known years ago, that he felt as if he wanted to tell her.

"The Gundersons?" she asked.

"No—I—well, I thought I might stop by and see Bryce."

Something passed through her gaze that he couldn't identify. "You were good friends?" she asked, without expression.

He swallowed. "No, actually. Not at all. In fact I—well, I just never liked him much. But that's partly why I—"

"You came to see his folks?"

"No. I wanted to see *him*, if he still lives around here anywhere."

Again, something seemed to pass through her gaze. "You didn't ever hear then?" she asked.

"Hear what?" He felt a shiver on the back of his neck.

"Bryce died a long time ago."

The shiver turned to ice. "*Died?*"

"Years ago, not too long after you left here," she said. "You never heard about it at all?"

"Never," he answered, still recovering from the blow. "What—what happened?"

"An automobile accident. He had joined the army and was just about to be sent to Viet Nam when it happened."

"That's terrible," he found himself saying. And it occurred to him that it was terrible not only for Bryce, but for himself—since there would be no way now to change things, no way to apologize or make amends.

"But you really hadn't liked him," she started.

"Well," he began, feeling embarrassed, "we just hit it off wrong—right from the time I moved here. But—"

"And I think you liked Sharilyn Tebbs, too," she put in quietly.

"Oh, I did," he answered quickly. "Yes, I did. And that just made things worse." Suddenly he stopped. "Did he finally marry her or—"

"Oh, no," she said. "They ended up marrying different people. Sharilyn married a guy from St. George the summer she graduated."

His mind flashed back to the dance and the image of Sharilyn in the light blue dress reaching up in order to dance with her towering partner.

"Well, what about you?" he asked. "You live over there?" He pointed to the little stone house with vines and hollyhocks behind her. He noticed then a young boy of ten or twelve sitting in the weeds beyond. "Is that your boy?"

She nodded, but he thought that, even in the failing light, he detected a blush or some slight uneasiness in her face. And then his eye caught the hand holding the flowers against her breast, and he noticed there was no ring on her finger.

He winced, feeling awkward. Poor Zinnie. He should have known. Far from being one of the "wild" girls, she had always been much more of a wallflower. Again the dance came to his mind, but before he could interpret what he saw, it faded. No, Zinnie Stokes had been the butt of more than one joke in those school years, and now he found it sad but not totally surprising that she had been taken advantage of in the years that had followed. Why was it that some people seemed doomed to be victimized?

He felt uncomfortable and looked back awkwardly to where Shawn was playing near the car. "That's *my* boy there. He's six." He hesitated a moment, then decided to go on, "My wife died this last January. Cancer."

"I'm sorry," she said softly. "Is that—is he your only child?"

He nodded. "He's been great company to me," he went on. "We're very close."

"I know how that is," she said, as if trying to smile.

The darkness seemed to be coming on quickly now, and he began to feel awkward standing there, talking over the fence.

"Well," he managed, "it's good to see you. It really is."

She seemed to blush and turned her head away nervously.

"You're looking great," he felt compelled to add. "Really."

"Well, I hope I've changed—some," she said quietly.

"Oh, you have," he put in quickly. Again the image of the dance flickered in his mind.

"You look just the same," she said. Then, as if embarrassed, she went on: "I could never remember your name for sure—Gavin Terry or Terry Gavin. No matter how I said it, it always seemed backwards."

"Well, you certainly remembered it tonight. And it felt good. You're the first person in Cedar City who has actually made me feel remembered."

She looked at him and seemed about to say something, but then she quickly made a move to go. "Well, it's nice to see you." She took a step or two backwards, looked over toward her son, and gave an awkward little nod and shrug.

"See you," he said, and raised one hand in a clumsy gesture of good-bye. But when he turned in the encroaching darkness, he felt very much alone. Bryce Gunderson was dead, had been dead for almost all the time he had been gone. Sharilyn had been married for twelve years or more to someone he had never actually met, and J. D.—

Darn! He had forgotten to ask about J. D. It almost made him want to turn back, and he did stop to look behind him at the lot across the fence, but he could see only that she had disappeared somewhere beyond the other side of the little house where her son had been. A dog barked somewhere in the neighborhood. A screen door slammed, and somewhere someone was still practicing finger exercises on the piano.

"Well, boy," he said to Shawn, "can you even see what you're doing?"

"Uh-uh," he grunted, still squatting by the ditch. "Well, sorta. I'm pretending there's a bunch of boats going down the river in a jungle. And it's nighttime and—"

"It *is* nighttime," Gavin said. "No need to pretend that. In fact, it's bedtime."

Shawn stood up. "But can we come here again?"

"Oh, well, I suppose," Gavin said. He found himself glancing toward the little house with hollyhocks, still dark. Once again, from far away, a lone dog barked.

But there was something about the dance that wouldn't let go of him. And something about Zinnia Stokes. Something he couldn't quite bring back. Or maybe didn't quite want to bring back.

And then, almost out of nowhere, it came to him.

Five

Even after he turned off the bedside lamp, he lay on his back for a long time piecing together the mutilated fragments of that last year in Cedar City. It reminded him of when he had been ten or eleven and he and a schoolmate had found, near an incinerator behind the stores downtown, several torn portions of a movie apparently discarded by the Cedar Theater. He remembered how the two of them excitedly held the pieces up to the light and then for an hour or more strung them along the sidewalk in front of his house, trying to fit them all together, to reconstruct the original narrative and fill in the gaps.

It was like that now. Funny how he had not thought of Zinnie Stokes in years. *Zinnie, Zinnie, tall and skinny...* But he strained now to put the splintered memories into some order, some pattern.

Zinnia Stokes. Sometime in the fifth or sixth grade he must have heard the name. At least he recalled the chant: *Zinnie, Zinnie, tall and skinny, pull her tail and hear her whinny.* He could picture the older boys and even some of the girls running after the awkward farm girl as they tried to pull one of her long white braids. But the pale waif he remembered from those days seemed to bear little relationship to the woman with the haunting blue eyes and corn-silk hair that had talked so softly to him across the fence this evening.

As he tried to remember her then, everything about her seemed to have been bleached: her hair, her skin, even the ill-fitting hand-me-down dresses she wore. Had it not been for the occasional singsong tauntings shouted by some of the children on the schoolgrounds, she might never have been noticed at all. It was true she had been in the grade a year younger, but he doubted if even her own classmates had known her. In fact, from the beginning of junior high to his junior year in high school, he could hardly remember her at all. Had they moved away? Or had she always been there, pale and quiet, somewhere in the background?

But there was one image from that last year at Cedar High that kept coming back to him now as if it had been burned indelibly on his retina. He had gone into the student council room one night after school and found her crying quietly to herself while she wrote something in a spiral notebook. He hadn't recognized her at first; looking back on it now, he realized she was already at that time closer to becoming the woman he had talked to over the fence than the strange, little washed-out girl with pigtails from elementary school. She had begun to use a little make-up, he remembered that, and it had given her face some color and drawn attention to her pale blue eyes. The mascara had smeared, though, and he remembered thinking how she looked like some pathetic little clown.

He remembered hesitating awkwardly at the pencil sharpener or in front of a bookshelf, wondering whether to intrude or just go about his business. *Zinnie, Zinnie, tall and skinny* ... It was hard to think that someone had still been making fun of her.

Anything wrong? he had asked.

In his memory, it was as though she had not even heard; and when he asked a second time, she seemed to flinch almost as if someone had struck her. He couldn't remember now if she had answered right away, but it was almost as if she had looked up, embarrassed, and then gone back to sniffling and writing in her notebook. Had he asked again? Or moved toward her? For some reason he could see her looking up with eyes as nervous as they were sad, and he could hear her say, *It's nothing,* or maybe *It's okay.* But then, as if in a remembered dream where scenes shift abruptly without logic or transition, he recalled sitting across the table from her while she explained, hesitatingly, what had happened: she had missed the schoolbus, whether accidentally or on purpose he couldn't remember. Wait—it was coming back: she had deliberately stayed to work on the school paper, hoping to get a ride home with another person on the newspaper staff who lived four or five miles out of town as well. But the office had been empty, the meeting evidently cancelled without anyone telling her, and when she had called home for a ride her father had scolded her for missing the bus.

It was hard for Gavin to remember why he had not given her a ride home. Maybe he had not yet got his driver's license, or maybe he had ridden to school on his bicycle. Or maybe he hadn't wanted to be seen by any of his friends riding in a car with odd little Zinnie Stokes— but he tried hard not to think about that now.

But the Preference Ball was the memory that hurt the most. He turned on his side in the double bed and looked out through the motel window at the red and yellow light blinking across the way. Zinnie Stokes. What had she called herself tonight while she stood there holding the flowers? Zin? The note, as he remembered it, had said Zinnia Stokes; and he felt his stomach knot up as he remembered it.

Hey, is this a joke or what?

Lemme see.

He uncrumpled the note and they read it together, J. D. pronouncing the words aloud: *Gavin Terry: If somebody has not already asked you to go to the Preference Ball, would you consider going with me? Zinnia Stokes.*

Zinnia Stokes! J. D. hooted and started to turn away with the note.

Hey, gimme that.

Zinnia Stokes! J. D. held the note high over his head. *Whoopee!*

C'mon. Give it to me. I wouldn't even have shown it to you if—

D'ya wanna frame it?

Hey, c'mon! He snatched at the note and it tore.

Oh, now look what you did! You could've put that in your scrapbook!

He crumpled up the two pieces. *Hey, get serious. What am I going to do?*

That's your problem, Romeo. You can always put a sack over her head.

Hey, c'mon. She's not that bad—but still, there's no way I can really go with her.

Tell her you broke your foot. Or tell her somebody else asked you first.

How can I?

Hey, don't sweat it. Somebody's sure to ask you.

And someone had. Funny how he couldn't remember who it was. Vickie, probably, or that girl named Kathleen. But what had always stuck in his mind was how Sharilyn had looked when he happened to glance across the floor and see her in the crowd with the tall, dark guy from St.

George. Before the dance, there had been some consolation in the fact that, even if she hadn't asked him, she had not asked J. D. or Bryce Gunderson either. But when he saw her that night in the pale blue dress, the light catching the sparkle from the Turkish earrings he had given her whenever she turned her head and her silky hair fell softly away from her cheek, something in him had wept.

For years, even after he had met Lois and fallen in love with her, the image would still come back, as available to him as any treasured photograph in any album—a memorial to that first, young, impossible love. But what startled him now was the realization that he had been skipping a page in that souvenir scrapbook of his mind. Almost as if it had been long ago torn out, he had ceased to miss it or to wonder about it. Strange, he thought, how our memory accommodates the pleasant, driving out the distasteful.

He tried now to find that page, to stare at it until the image, faded and suffering from neglect, began to emerge once more. Part of the old pain returned with it, but as he lay there, staring through the window at the flashing neon, he forced himself to bring back as much of the memory as he could.

Zinnia Stokes. He had avoided seeing her for days. How many? Two or three? A week? And then, when he knew that he could put it off no longer, he had deliberately looked for her in the halls, but it had been two or three more days before he finally found her.

He couldn't remember if they were in a hallway, a classroom, or in front of the school, but he could see her now, her head lowered a little, her eyes darting almost everywhere but directly at him. He couldn't remember if he had just been asked that day by someone else to go to the dance or if he had still been hoping at that time that someone would ask him. But he remembered lying to her—something about having already been asked weeks before—and apologizing for not having told her sooner.

It's okay, she had said, looking embarrassed and hurt. And then she had said something like *I wasn't really planning on it, anyway*, or *I didn't really think it was going to work out.* And then she had made a motion to move sideways a little, as if trying to slip away—an image that came back to him now with uncanny vividness—and he found himself saying now, in case he hadn't said it then, "I'm real sorry. I really am."

He rolled over, away from the lights that went on blinking outside the motel window, then he slipped his arm gently around Shawn's sleeping form. The little guy had asked to go back to the street where the Gundersons and now Zinnie Stokes lived, so why not? He wanted to ask Zinnie—Zinnia? Zin?—if she knew anything about J. D.; and he knew now that, as much as any of the things on his list of amends, he owed her an apology. And he lay there for a long time watching the flickering patterns reflected on the wall until he finally fell asleep.

Six

It was sunny but cool the next morning as they took a walk, then ate bacon and eggs at a new little roadside cafe. It cheered Gavin that one of the waitresses remembered him, even though she had been considerably younger than him, and he felt good that an older couple in a pickup, pulling up in front just as he and Shawn were leaving the cafe, not only recognized him but wanted to know all about his parents and how they were.

He felt good as they drove to the south part of town and parked in front of Hansens' Grocery. For a moment the store looked as if it were still closed, but just as he was about to feel the first pangs of disappointment, two children in swimming trunks emerged with popsicles.

"Guess what we're going to do in here," he said to Shawn.

"Get popsicles?"

"Well, not exactly. Although I guess we could do that too," he answered. "What I need to do here is pay back some money I owe."

"You owe them money?"

"Not much—but a long, long time ago, when I was

just a few years older than you, I came in here to buy something—a popsicle maybe—and Mr. Hansen was awfully busy. It seemed like he was trying to wait on three or four customers at once, and—"

"So didn't you pay?"

"Oh, I paid. And I remember that whatever it was I bought just cost a dime." He could still see himself standing on one foot and then the other waiting to pay the quarter he held in his sweaty palm. He remembered how Mr. Hansen would laugh and say something personal to each customer as he tallied up figures on a scrap of butcher paper or rang up sales on the old ornate register.

"So what happened?"

He could still feel the weight of the coins as they were dropped in his hand while Mr. Hansen called out, "Okay, who's next?"

"Well, what I think happened was this: I gave Mr. Hansen a quarter, but he was so busy helping other customers that he must have got mixed up and ended up giving me change for a dollar—ninety cents—instead of the fifteen cents I had coming."

"So what did you do?"

He could feel himself almost wanting to groan aloud. It was as if he were the child and his six-year-old interrogator were now the adult. "Well, what *should* I have done?" he finally asked.

"Give it back—right?"

"Right," he answered. Again, the inward groan. "But I didn't."

"You didn't?" Shawn asked incredulously.

"I didn't. And I don't know why. Maybe it was just that I was so startled and overwhelmed by the weight of all those coins in my hand that I walked away looking at them and thinking, 'Wow! I've hit the jackpot!'" He hesitated for a moment, studying the look on Shawn's face.

"You have to remember that I didn't go to Primary like you did—although my parents did teach me honesty and how to tell right from wrong. But I just looked at all those coins—nickels and dimes and quarters—and I walked out of there feeling really rich."

"So what did you do with them?"

"I can't even tell you. I mean, I don't remember. All I *do* remember is that I started feeling not so good about that money. In fact, I started feeling awful."

"So you took it back?"

Another groan from inside. *Oh, please,* he wanted to say, *stop being so grown-up about all this. Who's teaching who?* "No, strangely enough," he finally answered. "I don't know if it was because I really wanted to keep it so bad or if it was because I was embarrassed that I had walked out of there with it in the first place. At any rate, I never took it back. Never. But I also never forgot about it."

"So, let's take it back," Shawn said simply.

"Hey," Gavin returned, "good idea! Actually, that's why we're here. I've carried that around on my conscience for twenty years, and I'm here now to finally get rid of it."

"I'll go pay it back for you, if you want," Shawn offered.

"What do you say we both go?"

So they went into the store, the two of them, and Gavin found himself awestruck at how little had changed. The cash register was different, the old one unfortunately having been replaced by a more modern gray one, but the shelves, the meat counter, and even Mr. Hansen, bustling around with cartons of Rice Krispies, looked almost the way he remembered.

"I don't know if you remember me at all," Gavin began, "but— "

The white-haired man in the butcher apron stared at him intently as he set down his boxes. "Oh, but I do," he suddenly came back enthusiastically. "Sure I do. You might have to help me out with your name, but—"

"Gavin Terry—and this is my boy Shawn."

"What a lady-killer!" he said, reaching out his big hand to take Shawn's small one. "Gavin Terry. Sure. Your dad was the head supervisor of the forest service, right?"

Gavin nodded, glad to be back in his old neighborhood, and, as Hansen talked on and on, his mind drifted from time to time to all the afternoons he had stopped by for a root beer or Milky Way. When he had finally brought Hansen up to date on his life, including his joining the Church and Lois's death, he pulled a dollar bill from his billfold.

"Mr. Hansen," he began, "here's something I owe you."

"For what?"

"For keeping some wrong change you gave me about twenty years ago."

"Twenty years ago!" The old man laughed.

"Something like that." Gavin tried to smile. "It's one of those things, you know, that keep hanging over your head. Not a big thing, maybe, but a weight nevertheless. I'm just glad I could finally come back here and make it right."

Hansen seemed both amused and bewildered. "Twenty years—I can't believe it. Hey, go on—keep it."

Gavin dropped the bill on the counter. "Nah, you keep it. We're square now, okay?"

"Hey, wait a minute," Hansen insisted. "Take something for your boy. A couple of Twinkies—whatever. Okay?"

Gavin hesitated, glancing down at Shawn, then back at Hansen. "Well, how about a cherry popsicle?" he finally said.

"Cherry popsicle—fine!" Hansen echoed, wiping his hands on his apron.

"How about lime?" Shawn murmured quietly.

"Lime!" Gavin corrected, raising his voice.

Hansen smiled and fished out a pale green popsicle from the frozen foods bin. "Lime it is! Hey, Gavin. It's good to see you. And good to see this boy." He looked at them both, his face still in a big grin. "I can't believe it: two thousand miles to pay back a few nickels. You're great, Gavin. Your dad's great, you know that?" he said, coming over to squeeze Shawn's shoulder.

And he felt great, after they had both shaken the old man's hand, said their good-byes, and stepped once again into the morning sunshine. *Okay, world,* he felt like saying. *What's next? I'm ready to handle anything.* He honestly did feel as though there was nothing on his list he feared, nothing that would even make him hesitate. But something told him he had better move quickly while he was still on such a "high"—for fear the elation would not last forever.

It was still with him as they drove toward the little stone house where Zinnia Stokes had been, but he felt the first slight dampening of his spirits when they passed slowly by the house. He couldn't quite put his finger on it: there was a faint air of forlornness, of neglect, even abandonment. He made a U-turn at the corner, looked at his watch—not quite ten o'clock—and drove slowly past the house one more time. There was something heavily nostalgic about the honey-colored stone as well as the pink and lavender hollyhocks along the front and the three tall poplar trees out back. But there was also something more than merely old-fashioned about it—something melancholy, even sad. As he glanced back over his shoulder in one last attempt to pinpoint what it was, he noticed that one half of the tiny front lot behind the weathered picket fence was overgrown with weeds.

It suddenly occurred to him that, although he saw no

signs of life about, Zinnie Stokes might be watching them from the window as they passed back and forth in front of her house. Embarrassed, he turned around in the middle of the block and drove back, pulling to a stop in front of her place.

"What are we doing?" Shawn asked, his lips chartreuse from the dripping popsicle in his hand.

"Recognize this place? This is where we were last night. But stay here in the car for a few minutes while I check to see if anyone's home. Okay?"

He left the car and, passing through the creaking picket gate, followed the sidewalk to the front door. *I'll ask first if she can tell me for sure where J. D. is*, he thought to himself, *and then ...* But he wasn't quite sure what he would say then, and once again he found himself feeling nearly the same kind of relief he had felt last night when no one had answered at the Gunderson house. He knocked one last time, then went back to the car, puzzled by the abundance of weeds growing near the walk.

"Can't I play here?" Shawn wanted to know.

"Later, maybe," he replied. "But right now, how would you like to go with me to pay another debt?"

"You owe more money?" Shawn asked, aghast.

"I hate to say it, but I think I do," Gavin answered, going on to explain about Mrs. Mendenhall and the yard-cleaning job when he had been fourteen.

Whether she had approached him or whether he had happened to knock on her door while going around the neighborhood soliciting odd jobs, he couldn't quite recall. But he did remember the agreement: he would clean up her backyard, picking up all the old scraps of lumber and wire from a run-down chicken coop and long-abandoned pigpen, so that an elderly neighbor who had offered his pickup truck might haul it away. The job, he figured, would take two or three Saturday mornings; and she had offered him fifteen dollars to do it.

At first it had gone well. He could remember how fast the first few hours went and how much he had accomplished—moving barrels and part of an old tractor, taking apart the tangle of chicken wire and weathered boards that had once been a coop, and rescuing odds and ends of an old washing machine and an outboard motor that had been almost swallowed up in dead leaves and weeds and all the tall, green grass.

But then the old man Staheli—it was Staheli, wasn't it?—had come by that next Saturday afternoon to pick it up on his way to the dump. The two of them had loaded everything that was ready to go into the pickup while storm clouds gathered gloomily overhead. He remembered how Mrs. Mendenhall had come out to thank old Mr. Staheli and how she had turned to him then and given him the fifteen dollars, even though he had said there was more left to do. Part of the pigpen still needed to be torn apart and a few things straightened up, but, in view of the oncoming rain and Mr. Staheli's anxiousness to take what was already a full load to the dumpground, they had agreed that he would finish the rest on the following Saturday.

What had happened? More rain? Or was that the week of that first unexpected snowfall, followed by months of cold, stormy weather? Then spring came, and for days on end he would forget about it, although the thought of it still hovered over him from time to time and came at odd moments to haunt him. Now, more than fifteen years later, the specter was still there; only now, he hoped, he would have the chance to exorcise it once and for all.

He had to drive up and down four or five blocks before he found the house. It seemed smaller than he remembered, and the fence had been taken down, but he recognized the cluster of plum trees and lilac bushes surrounding the property.

They had to ring the doorbell several times, but finally the door opened a crack, and a much older and shriveled version of Mrs. Mendenhall peeked out.

"Mrs. Mendenhall?" he began quickly. "I'm Gavin Terry. Remember me?"

She shook her head, her eyes darting quickly from his face to his feet and then falling, it seemed, on Shawn.

"Gavin Terry. We used to live here years ago. I'm the one that cleaned your yard for you. Took down the chicken coop and—"

Her mouth opened a little and her eyes fixed themselves on his face. "Oh, my," she said. "That was a long time ago."

"Yes," he agreed. "About fifteen or sixteen years ago. But I've never forgotten—because—well, because I really didn't ever finish the job the way I said I would."

She looked nervous but seemed to be trying to locate a smile. "Oh, my goodness, I can't even remember. It's gone now, though. The chicken coop's long gone."

"I know, but I had promised to take down the rest of the little fence that used to be a pigpen and I—"

"Gone," she said. "All gone now. Long ago." She narrowed her eyes as if trying to think. "But—I don't—forgive me, I'm old—but I'm afraid I don't know what it is you want."

"I'm sorry," he apologized. "It's just that I've always felt bad about not doing the job right. I took the money— fifteen dollars—and always intended to come by and finish up the rest, but I'm afraid I never did." She continued to stare at him, the faint trace of a smile creeping along her wrinkled chin and cheek. He hurried on, "You must think I'm absolutely crazy, but it's something that has bothered me for years. Mrs. Mendenhall, I'd like to give you back some of that money. Or maybe—"

She raised a quivering hand and muttered something followed by a nervous little laugh. "Didn't do your job, did you? Well," she said, looking down at Shawn, "what do we do about that? I really can't remember, although—although, maybe, yes—I think one winter we did have quite a pile of stuff that never got hauled away. But I don't remember so well anymore. I'm going to be ninety-one, do you know that?"

"Ninety-one," he repeated. "Incredible! You seem to be very alert and able to get around pretty well."

"Oh, not so good, not so good, I'm afraid," she said, waving her trembling hand again.

"Then is there something we can do for you? Something you need done?"

"Oh, I don't think . . ." she said, her voice trailing off. But then she seemed to stare off into nowhere. Suddenly she looked down at Shawn. "What about this little man? How is he? Is he a good worker?" She cackled from somewhere deep in her throat. "I suppose the two of you could help me bring up a few things from the basement. I can't get up and down the steps, you know, and Delmar was supposed to do it, but he's got him a job now up north, and who knows when I'll . . ." Again her voice trailed off as she scooted herself around to face back into the house. Then she reached out to grasp the doorframe and shuffled her slippered feet so that she could turn around and look at them again. "Can you come back?"

"Of course. Whenever you say," he said anxiously.

"Then come back. Let me get my head working. There's two or three things I've been wanting, and everything's such a—such a mess down there, and here I am, I can't get up or down and—"

"Fine. Why don't we come tomorrow? Maybe tomorrow morning—and we'll be prepared to work, won't we, Shawn? We can move things around for you, even straighten up your basement if you want."

"I'm afraid you'll need a flashlight down there," she mumbled. "There's a light, but I think the globe's all burned out."

"I'll bring you a new globe, okay? We'll do whatever needs doing down there. Is that okay?"

She shook her head, accompanied by a low, throaty cackle. "I suppose so," she said, the head-shaking evolving into a quivering nod. Then she smiled at them. "Can't have you toting a burden of guilt around, can we?" She snickered and reached out to pat his arm. "All right, then," she mumbled, starting to scoot herself back around, "you come back then and we'll see . . ." She turned back and smiled one last time as she slowly pulled the door closed.

Gavin sighed and pulled Shawn in against him as they started down the walk. "Well, that worked out pretty well, huh? Better than I thought."

Shawn looked up and nodded. "But will it be all spidery and scary down there?" he asked.

"I hope not. But we're brave, aren't we?"

"Sort of," Shawn murmured unconvincingly.

They drove down Main Street, got directions at a gas station to Woodruff Shipley's, then searched out the house in the north part of town. A teenaged granddaughter told them he had gone fishing with her dad but she expected them back sometime in the late afternoon. They drove then to find his parents' friends, the Bigelows, and discovered that Fred Bigelow had died two years before, and Clea Bigelow, her hair white now, was temporarily bedridden with a broken hip. Her daughter-in-law from Denver fixed them all lunch, and the three of them talked while Shawn played by himself in their backyard.

He was disappointed that Mrs. Bigelow didn't have much information about J. D. Sargent or Vickie Cameron or any of the others he asked about—"You just lose track of them all, I'm afraid," she said—and the name Zinnia Stokes, when he decided to casually bring it up, meant nothing to her. "Of course," she told him, "a lot of families live on farms around here that I don't even know."

And so, while the afternoon sun seemed to lull much of the town into a sluggish siesta, he and Shawn drove around the back streets and then watched the Utah Shakespeare Company rehearsing *Romeo and Juliet* on the outdoor stage among the pine trees. Shawn finally stretched out on the lawn for a nap, and for a few minutes, Gavin too dozed in the cool afternoon shade.

When he woke up, a kind of restlessness, even a surprising sense of urgency, made him anxious to drive once more by Zinnia Stokes's little stone house. It would be good, he told himself, to not leave that dangling, but to clear it up while it was fresh on his mind.

But the house looked as quiet as ever when they pulled up in front, and when he knocked several times on the door, it still gave off the air of being neglected and deserted. He knocked one last time, then, without wanting to seem too forward, tried to look into one of the windows.

The house was empty.

The knowledge startled him, even though he realized that, from the first time they came by that morning, he must have already come to half-suspect it. Bolder now, he stepped close to the window and looked again. Through the lace curtains he could see that there was some furniture. But what was it that made the house seem so obviously uninhabited? Dust on the bare hardwood floor, a piece of cardboard propped up against the opening of the fireplace, the naked mantel flanked by barren bookshelves . . .

He glanced next door. If the Gundersons were gone as she had said, there would be no chance of information there. He looked to the right. Beyond the trees he could see a brick home, and, if he was not mistaken, someone was moving past the window.

He left Shawn trying to float a crushed pop can down the grassy ditch, and went to the house next door. Someone immediately answered the bell, and he found himself facing a middle-aged woman with well-groomed platinum hair.

"Yes?" she asked.

"Excuse me," he said, "but I was wondering about the people next door. I'm looking for a—a Zinnia Stokes."

"A what?" The lady tipped her head sideways as if she had heard wrong.

"Zinnia Stokes." But he could see that it hadn't helped. "A woman about thirty-ish, with a young boy. I thought she lived next door."

The lady made a little face of bewilderment, and he saw her shoulders shrug a little. "Where? Over there?" she pointed. "Nobody lives over there. In fact, no one has lived there the whole time we've been here."

For a moment he couldn't think of what to say. Finally, "How long has that been?"

"A little over a year. We moved here from California about fifteen months ago, and it's been empty all that time."

He swallowed. There seemed to be nothing more to say, nothing more he could ask, and yet he felt reluctant to leave without more information of some kind.

"You know," he found himself saying, "I came by here the other night—last night, in fact. A woman was in the yard there, with long blonde hair and her arms full of flowers, and she told me—she told me she lived there."

He could still see the way the setting sun had cast a golden-pink glow over her pale skin and corn-silk hair. There had been something about her, something so fresh and natural in her eyes and her cheeks and the way she held the deep pink flowers against her that she seemed to have wandered away from some nineteenth-century tapestry of Old-World peasants.

"You didn't see anyone like that?" he asked again.

The California woman in the doorway shook her head, looking more puzzled than ever. "I wish I could help you, but I can't even imagine who it would have been. I honestly have never seen anyone around that little house all the time we've been here. I don't even know who owns it."

He looked back toward the little stone house, feeling unexpectedly empty and disappointed. "All right then," he finally said. "Sorry to have troubled you."

"Sorry," she said, tipping her head sideways and managing a smile.

He walked back toward the car and stood for a long time looking at the deserted little house, a few vines clinging haphazardly to the dusty-amber stone. Why hadn't he asked more last night? Why hadn't he given her some indication that he would come back? He had known then, hadn't he, even before he left her, that he wanted to return?

He glanced at Shawn, who still crouched on the ditch-bank, dropping stick canoes into the miniature Amazon, then he walked close to the picket fence and peeked over, looking for some stray pair of scissors or clippers, even some telltale leaves that might have fallen to the ground, or the actual bed of flowers from which she had picked her bouquet. But there was nothing—only a few stray hollyhocks growing up from the tangle of grass and weeds that surrounded the house.

The whole thing was strangely like a dream. He remembered seeing an old movie on TV in which some ethereally lovely girl would appear, disappear, then reappear in an abandoned lighthouse on the rocky cliffs overlooking the sea. He felt a little shiver along the back of his neck.

Seven

As they drove slowly away from the little house, Shawn stretched himself out on the seat and yawned two or three times as he tried to get through a verse of "Down in the Valley." Gavin mumbled something half to himself, half aloud.

"Who are you looking for, Dad?" he heard Shawn ask.

"A lady," he murmured. "Do you remember that lady last night standing by the fence with all the flowers?"

"Uh-uh," Shawn answered, indifferently. Then, "Well, sorta. Anyway, I heard you talking to someone."

Suddenly he found himself craning his neck forward and peering intently through the windshield. Down the road about half a block was a woman with long blonde hair walking in the shade of the cottonwoods beside a little boy.

"I think I just found her," he muttered aloud and accelerated the car in order to reach them before they disappeared into one of the houses along the way.

But something seemed not quite right as he pulled up alongside them. The hair seemed to be a darker blonde, the woman younger, and the boy much smaller than he remembered. The girl, probably only in her early twenties, stopped and looked at him as he stared at her from within the car.

Embarrassed, he leaned over and unrolled the window on Shawn's side. "I'm sorry, but—do you know where I would find Zinnia Stokes?"

The girl with the little boy bent down enough to see inside the car as she came a few steps closer. "Who?"

"Zinnia Stokes."

"Zinnia Stokes," she repeated, frowning. "Is she a student at the college?"

"No. She's about twenty-nine or thirty, has a little boy about ten or so."

She looked puzzled. "I'm sorry. We've lived around here for four or five years, but I've never heard of anyone by that name. Stokes, is it?" She shrugged. "You'd probably better look in the phone book."

The phone book. Why hadn't he thought of that? If she had never married, she would be in there under her own name; and, in any case, the parents would more than likely still be listed.

He nodded his thanks to the young lady on the sidewalk and drove back toward Main Street, watching, as he went, for a telephone booth. Finally spotting one near a gas station, he got out, found the telephone book, and immediately began searching the pages for the name Stokes.

There was nothing.

Hoping he had browsed over the names too hastily, he went down the list more carefully; still there was nothing. What did that mean? He knew they had lived on a farm, but was it far enough away that it was actually listed under a neighboring community?

For a while he stood near the phone booth staring off toward the blur of cars coming and going down the main street. Then he went back to where Shawn lolled on the front seat with his head hanging down to the floor.

"Did you find her?" he asked, still hanging upside down.

"Not yet," Gavin answered. "But I think I have an idea."

He drove back to the north end of town, where he sought out once again the large rambling brick home that was the Shipley residence. A faded big boat of a car was in the driveway, a fishing pole propped against each side like two spindly oars. Around the side of the house, sitting on the steps of a small porch with white Victorian trim, was the heavy, bald-headed man he remembered as Mr. Shipley. His sleeves were rolled up, and, as Gavin drew nearer, he saw that he was busily cleaning trout and dropping them into a green plastic pan.

"Mr. Shipley," he said hesitantly, pulling Shawn in beside him.

The old fellow looked up.

"You probably don't remember me," Gavin went on, "but I used to go to school here—"

"Of course you did! Come on over here and let me have a good look at you. Gavin, wasn't it?"

"That's right," he returned quickly, feeling pleased. "Gavin Terry."

"Well, how are you? Is this your boy?"

"Sure is. This is Shawn. He's going to be a second-grader next fall."

Mr. Shipley made an awkward motion with his hands, slimy-wet and slightly bloody from the fish. "Excuse me for not shaking your hand, but you caught me right in the middle of this mess." He smiled warmly at Gavin. "So what brings you back out this way? You people moved back East, didn't you? A long time ago."

"Right. I didn't even get to finish my senior year here. But I remember well the classes I had from you. I'm surprised you still remember me, though." He sat down on the edge of a wicker lawn chair and again pulled Shawn in beside him.

"Well," Shipley began, chuckling to himself, "after several thousand students, you sure as heck can't remember them all. But, for some reason, I do remember you. That's been ten years or so, hasn't it?"

"More. Actually about fourteen, I guess, since I took English from you." He hesitated a moment while Shipley mumbled something about "fourteen years" and shook his head, then he went on, "Actually, part of the reason I'm here is—is to straighten up something about that class."

Shipley stopped cutting away at one of the fish and looked at him, then went on, less vigorously.

"You see, I don't know if you remember or not, but we read *Macbeth* that year, and I wrote a paper—which you read aloud, by the way, in the class." Again Gavin found himself hesitating. "Anyway, I'm embarrassed to say that I—well, all those ideas weren't exactly original. I mean, I copied a lot of it from a book I found."

Again Shipley stopped for a moment, then smiled a little. "Not many sophomores have very original ideas, I'm afraid," he said. "Are you trying to say you didn't give sources for your material?"

"I guess that's what it amounted to. It wasn't as if I was quoting any famous critics or anything like that. I just simply lifted three or four paragraphs from this one book, if I remember right. I agreed with the ideas and felt I couldn't say them any better, so I just copied them down." He felt uncomfortable, for both Shawn and Mr. Shipley were looking at him.

"You know," Shipley began after a little pause, "I think

I almost remember that paper. And if you say I read it aloud, I may well have done it just to see what reaction it would get in the class. Sometimes the student himself will fall apart, and sometimes another student will bring up something about the diction or the sentence structure and how it sounds—well—borrowed."

"You read it, all right, and I think I died a thousand times. But no one seemed to catch on. A lot of guys just razzed me about being a brain or trying to impress you or something."

"You *were* bright, no doubt about that. You probably could have written a paper as good as that one on your own."

"I think I *could* have, I honestly do!" Gavin put in hurriedly. "That's just it. I don't know why I felt like I had to borrow all that. I liked the play and I—"

"Maybe you learned something by it all," Shipley suggested.

"Oh, I'm sure I did. Having you read it in class devastated me—and I wished a thousand times that everything you were reading had been my own. Anyway," and he found himself hesitating, "I—I don't know what can be done now." He shifted uneasily in the chair, surprised how he suddenly felt like a sixteen-year-old student again. "I just wanted to, once and for all, clear that all up and—and tell you, I guess, that it was not an honest paper and I'm—I'm truly sorry about that."

"You know," Shipley began, "I guess I probably suspected that at the time, and I guess I could have even flunked you—"

"You should have," Gavin cut in. "I deserved it."

"But I must have had some faith in you and in your writing. I really can't remember why I let it go, to tell you the truth. But I do know one thing."

"What's that?"

"Your coming here sort of restores my faith in humanity." Shipley put down his knife and rested his elbows on his knees, smiling at them. "I mean it. The fact that you would take the time—" He stopped, then asked quickly, "Where do you live now, anyway? Are you around here anywhere?"

"Not really," Gavin said, blushing. "We're living in Ohio. My wife passed away a few months ago, and I just decided Shawn and I would come out here for a little vacation and, well, maybe straighten up a few old scores. Nothing all that serious, but—"

"I can't believe it," Shipley said, shaking his head. "I'm sorry to hear about your wife, genuinely sorry. But I feel so good about your taking the time to come back and—"

"That's what everybody's said," Gavin broke in. "They've been great. I'm just sorry I let it go—for so long."

"Hey, would you stay and have some fried fish and hot biscuits with us?"

"We'd like to," Gavin said quickly, "but I really think we ought to move along. There's a couple of people I'm anxious to see, and I'm afraid I might miss them."

"Are you leaving right away?"

"Well, not *right* away, but there are a couple of things I'm sort of anxious to take care of."

"Anything I can do to help?"

"Well, actually yes, maybe. For one thing, I had hoped to locate J. D. Sargent."

"Sargent—J. D. Sargent. You mean DeLyle's boy?"

"That's right. We were pretty close, but I'm afraid I've completely lost track—"

Shipley tilted his head sideways and called over his shoulder, "Reva! Whatever became of Millie and DeLyle's boy, J. D.? Is he the one that went down to Vegas? Or is he down in St. George?"

A plump woman in a housedress and apron came to the screen door and opened it wide enough to nod her greetings to them. "J. D., you say? He wasn't the one that became a doctor, was he? Or was that Kelvin?"

"Kelvin, I think, is the doctor. J. D., if I remember right, is the one that married that girl from over to Fillmore or somewhere and opened up a real-estate business in St. George. Isn't that right?"

Mrs. Shipley nodded slowly, wiping her hands on her apron.

"This is Gavin Terry, Mother," Shipley explained. "And his boy. All the way from Ohio—can you believe it? I asked them to stay for supper, but I guess they've got things they've got to do."

"There *was* one other thing," Gavin put in hurriedly. "One other person I wondered about." He hesitated, uncomfortable that the name he was about to say might still have the old connotations of the strange and straggly little girl from the farm. "I wondered if you could tell me anything about Zinnia Stokes."

Mrs. Shipley was calling something back into the house, and Shipley, as though unable to catch the name leaned forward, his elbows still resting on his knees, and tipped his head sideways as though one ear were better than another.

"Stokes," Gavin repeated, uneasily. "Zinnia Stokes."

Shipley shrugged. "I don't remember the name, I'm afraid. Stokes, you say?"

Gavin found himself repeating the name silently. Surely he had it right. *Zinnie Stokes chews and smokes, Gets her kicks from old Cowpokes.*

Suddenly he was aware that Shipley was talking, but then he saw that he was looking back toward his wife. "Stokes? Know any Stokeses?"

"There was that family that used to live out in the valley, out toward Enoch," she started to say.

"That's it, I'm sure," Gavin put in quickly. "Zinnia Stokes."

"Right," Mrs. Shipley agreed. "Zinnia Stokes." But then her expression changed. "She died, I'm afraid."

"Died?" he heard himself saying.

"Oh yes, three or four years ago. And then the old man Stokes, he sold the farm, I think, and moved away. I really didn't know the family, but—"

A beating in his temples blocked out her voice, and he found himself pushing Shawn away enough so he could steady himself and get up from the wicker chair.

The whole thing was too uncanny.

In his mind he saw her once again standing on the other side of the fence like someone who had wandered there from another place, another time. Once again he saw the flowers resting against her shoulder and the creamy whiteness of her neck. He saw the clear, pale skin, the hair, clean and shining, and the eyes with their strange, smoky blueness.

"I'm sorry," Mrs. Shipley was saying. "Did you know them very well?"

"No, " his voice came echoing back to his ears. "No, not really," and he suddenly felt drained and very dizzy—as though the long grueling drive from Ohio to Utah had finally caught up with him.

Eight

When he left the Shipleys, he found himself driving almost aimlessly out of town. At first he started south, but then, not sure he was ready quite yet to go to St. George, he turned east at J. C. Penney's and followed the road that led in the direction of Cedar Canyon.

"Now where are we going, Dad?" Shawn wanted to know.

"Just—just for a little ride, I guess. Nowhere in particular."

"Are you mad?"

"Mad? No, why?"

"You look sort of mad. Or worried."

"I'm just thinking. Trying to put things together."

"About Zinnia Strokes or whatever her name is?"

He swallowed. *Hey, kid,* he wanted to say. *What's with all this cross-questioning? Who's in charge here—me or you?* "That's part of it," he managed to say. Actually, more than part of it right now, he told himself. All of it. Why was he now so concerned with a person who had never meant anything to him? Had meant absolutely nothing, in fact. But more than that, what was the explanation for all that had transpired during the last twenty hours or so? Without question, Zinnia Stokes had been there, her arms full of flowers, standing on the other side of that fence just as the sun was going down. He grew impatient. Somewhere there was an explanation. But why did Mrs. Shipley think she had died? And why had she told him she lived in the little stone house when it had been closed up for at least a year or more? And why had—

"Dad," Shawn interrupted, kneeling on the front seat and turning to face him. "Dad, how come you did so many bad things when you were little?"

He cringed. "So many? Did I really do a lot?"

"It seems like it," Shawn answered, a touch of sadness or disappointment in his voice.

Gavin felt again the groaning inside. "I'm sorry, Shawn, if it seems like a lot." Was it wrong, he asked himself one more time, to have brought Shawn in on all of this? Of course, he hadn't told him about the election and about the Preference Ball and about his hatred of Bryce Gunderson and about many, many other things, and probably with good reason. There was really no need, was there? But about the English paper, the money at Hansens' Market, and—what else? Oh yes, the unfinished job at Mrs. Mendenhall's. He felt good thinking about that; at least, together, they could still work out that debt; and maybe, if Shawn could feel his earnestness, it would help redeem things, help ease the feeling he had now that he had been exposing a bad side of himself and possibly fallen considerably in the eyes of the little guy that now nestled beside him and rested his head against his arm.

"I guess I did two or three things that weren't as good as they should have been," he said soberly, "and I just want to make them right."

"You're a good dad," Shawn reassured him quietly.

He slipped one arm around the boy and pulled him in snugly against his side.

He tried to think about J. D. and how it would be if he went to St. George and searched him out. Not *if*, but *when*. Of course he would go; he *had* to go. But Bryce Gunderson—there was no way to make amends there, and maybe it was just as well. He cringed, pricked by feelings of guilt. With Bryce it had been something he had known he should do, yet could he have really—honestly—done it? With Zinnia—again he winced as the needles of guilt pricked sharply into him—with Zinnia, it was another matter: his heart ached to see her again, just for a moment, and to tell her that he was sorry, sorry for the way he had treated her and the way everyone had ever treated her. Just remembering her face and the softness in her eyes, he longed—yes, ached—to look across a fence and find her there once again the way she had been—and she really *had* been there, *must* have been there—the night before.

He slowed down as he came to a spot on the road where a little turnout allowed him to turn off, make a U-turn, and start down toward the town. No need going further up into the canyon, he told himself. Yet, where was he going? He felt nervous, impatient, frustrated. He knew he wanted to drive one more time past the little stone house with the vines and the hollyhocks. He would go there now, and he would go back again and again if he had to. Above all, he would be there when the sun went down, just to see if, by chance . . .

He glanced at his watch: four-thirty-three.

He looked up again and swerved just a little to the right as a car came around the curve. Better watch the road; the canyon drive had always been a little tricky, especially speeding down toward—

He jerked suddenly, jolted by what he had just seen.

"Incredible," he whispered as he stepped on the brake and pulled quickly over to the side of the road. It *was* incredible—but surely it was no vision, no mirage: sitting in the car that had just passed on its way up the canyon had been Zinnia Stokes.

He turned the car quickly around, feeling almost breathless. "Incredible," he said again.

Shawn looked up at him, then sat up and looked out the windshield. "What's happening? Why are we turning around so much?"

"I might be wrong," he said, stepping heavily on the gas pedal, "but I'm almost positive that Zinnia Stokes was in that car that just passed us."

Shawn leaned forward, holding onto the dashboard. "What car?"

"Up ahead, probably around that turn."

"But didn't she die?"

"Don't ask me. The whole thing's far too mixed up for me. But last night, that lady I talked to while you were playing along the ditchbank, that was Zinnia Stokes. And unless I'm seeing things, the person driving that car up ahead is the same one I talked to last night."

Zinnie, Zinnie, tall and skinny . . . What was the other one that had popped into his mind after years of being totally forgotten? Oh, yes: *Zinnie Stokes, chews and smokes.* The little jibes and mocking chants were painful to him now, and he wanted to obliterate them totally from his mind. But what about *her* mind? Had they already been obliterated there? Or were they embedded there forever?

He could see the car up ahead. He was gaining on it now, and he could even see the long, pale hair of the driver and the head of a small boy in the seat next to her. But something made him hesitate just a little: would it possibly turn out similar to the mistake he had made earlier when he thought he had seen Zinnie and her son walking down the street and it turned out not to be them at all? Was he going to cause a scene overtaking this car up ahead only to find out that two strangers were in it?

As he narrowed the gap between the two cars, he deliberated whether to honk the horn or to simply try to pass. The two-lane road was becoming steeper now and snaked its way treacherously between the tree-covered hills that rose up sharply on both sides. He settled on the honking, and began beating out a little "shave-and-a-hair-cut, six-bits" one-note melody on the horn with the palm of his hand.

He could see her turn her head and tip it slightly to look in the rearview mirror, but he still couldn't be absolutely sure it was Zinnie Stokes. Her son turned around on the seat—a bigger boy than he remembered—and stared out the rear window at them. Gavin honked out the tattoo one more time; again she tipped her head to the mirror, and again the boy twisted around and looked at them.

Not far ahead, he could see the turnout where he had made the first U-turn a few minutes earlier, and as he honked one more time, he motioned with his hand for her to turn off. She had slowed down considerably, but she seemed about to drive past the place where the road widened into a turnout until all of a sudden he saw her signal light blink two or three times and she pulled off. He eased his own car off the road, stopped immediately behind her, and got out.

It was her. She was rolling down her window and looking back over her shoulder with a look of bewilderment almost masking what seemed to be the trace of a strange smile.

He felt out of breath. "Zinnia—" he started.

"Zin," she corrected softly. "But what . . .?" And her words seemed to trail off and become lost, replaced by a kind of helpless shrug of her shoulders.

He leaned on the car, looked away, then back at her, taking a deep breath. "I don't know what's going on," he said, giving his head a little shake as if to clear it.

"What is it?" she asked, her voice sounding soft, innocent.

"They told me—they told me back in town that—that you had died three or four years ago," he began, experiencing, as he said the words, a feeling of warmth, of embarrassment, overtaking his face.

Her look grew more puzzled, then the brows relaxed. "They must mean my mother," she said. "My mother was Zinnia Stokes too—that's why I've generally just gone by Zin." She paused a moment, her pale blue eyes seeming to study him. "I'm sure they must have meant my mother. She died about four-and-a-half years ago."

He felt his whole body relax, but he felt as well the feeling of foolishness returning. Her mother—how stupid of him. Why hadn't he thought of that? But it still didn't explain the empty house.

"I thought you told me you lived in that house near the corner," he breathed. "The little one with the vines and the hollyhocks. But I went there today and it's—it's boarded up. I mean, no one has lived there for—"

"I'm sorry," she interrupted. "I guess I didn't bother to explain. We did live there—until Scott was about two and a half, I guess. Then he and I moved to Logan." She glanced back over her shoulder at the boy sitting in the seat beside her. "This is Scott. He's eleven."

"Hi, Scott."

"Hi," the boy answered, his voice quiet but polite.

"This is Gavin Terry," she explained to her son. "He and I went to high school about the same time."

"And that's my boy Shawn," Gavin said, tossing his head back to where Shawn sat peering out the windshield. "He's almost seven." He looked back at her, straining to see in the smoky-blue eyes a sign, any sign, of the skinny little girl with pigtails that had been the butt of so many cruel jokes. "So, are you in Cedar now?"

"Not really. Just for a visit. Our home's in Logan."

"Just—you and Scott?" he found himself interrupting, feeling somehow that he needed to know.

"Just the two of us," she answered. She looked away for a moment, and he thought he also detected a faint blush. "Scott's in school, of course, and I have a good job—working with emotionally handicapped children. It's all worked out quite well, actually."

He couldn't help looking at her, although he felt uncomfortable. Even without the flowers there was something fresh and almost woodsy about her skin, something even radiant. Why was it he had always pictured her as a child with bleached-white eyelashes and spattered with freckles?

"I drove back by your house today, and when I saw the place was all locked up and empty . . ."

"I'm sorry to have misled you. I was just over there last night picking some flowers and trying to pull a few weeds. There's a chance we might rent the place. Actually, it's been rented all along, up until about a year ago."

"I'm almost sorry—well—disappointed to find that you don't live there. Something about it seemed sort of—well, sort of right, somehow."

She seemed to blush again as she glanced quickly away, then back. "Maybe it's because we're both a little run-down—relics of the past," she said, seeming to be trying to smile.

He could feel himself blushing now. "I didn't mean that at all." But he didn't know how to explain what he did mean; the only words that came—old-fashioned, quaint—seemed not quite right. He found himself studying her: how would someone else describe her? Not exactly *pretty;* the word was too frivolous, too superficial. But certainly no longer *plain* . . . The only words he could summon up—words that had even entered his mind the night before—were words he himself didn't use, words like *lovely, haunting,* maybe *hauntingly lovely.*

He noticed that she seemed to shift uncomfortably under his gaze and that she had turned her eyes away and appeared to be fumbling nervously with the keys hanging from the ignition.

"I didn't mean to hold you up," he apologized. "You were probably in a hurry to go somewhere."

"Not really," she answered. "Well, a little, I suppose. We were on our way to Navajo Lake." She looked over at her son. "I had promised Scott we could camp one night at the lake, and we wanted to get there and get set up before dark."

Navajo Lake. It had been years since he had thought of it. Memories of autumn quaking aspen and crystal-clear waters flooded him. "You're on your way now?" he asked. "To camp at the lake?"

She cast a glance over her shoulder, and he noticed the sleeping bags stacked on the back seat. "It's just something I promised. We'll just stay overnight and cook our breakfast and maybe go for a canoe ride or something."

He could feel a tinge of envy seeping through him. "Sounds great," he said. "Wish we were doing the same."

She changed color, and he could hear the faint jingle of the car keys as she fidgeted with them.

"Maybe we'll have to do that—sometime before we go back," he went on quickly.

"And where is back?" she asked.

"To Ohio. We've been there a long time now, and it's—it's sort of home."

She smiled, then seemed to glance away a little nervously.

"Well, I won't hold you up any longer," he said. "I hope you—you can find a good camping spot and that you—that everything turns out great."

"Thanks," she said quietly. "It should be nice up there now, even though it's probably going to be a little cool at night."

"Looks like you've got great weather, though," he said, looking up at the clear blue of the afternoon sky. He stepped back from the car as she turned the key in the ignition and started up the engine.

He felt there was more he wanted to say—more even than the apology for the Preference Ball which he still wanted to make when the time seemed more right. *Maybe we'll see you up there*, he was almost tempted to say, but she was already slowly beginning to ease the car forward.

"Good-bye, then," she said, and her son too managed a little smile and gave a perfunctory wave of his hand.

What if we joined you— he felt on the verge of saying, but something held him back. He made a little motion with his hand instead. "Bye," he echoed. He checked the road to make sure no cars were coming and then motioned them on their way.

As he walked back to his car where Shawn played with the miniature *Star Wars* figures along the dashboard, he felt once again the emptiness he had felt the night before when he had gone back to the car and left her on the other side of the fence by the little stone house.

He hadn't even asked when they would be coming back to Cedar, or if they were coming back to stay at all. The back seat had been fairly loaded; maybe Navajo Lake was just one last stop before they went back to Logan. Stupid of him—why hadn't he asked?

"There they go! Zap 'em!" Shawn pronounced in his deepest voice, and Gavin looked up to see Han Solo and Princess Leia being scooted rapidly across the dashboard.

He leaned back and rested his head against the seat. It was still early. They could go back into town, get something to eat, maybe see what was on at the movie theater. He stared up through the windshield at the deep blue of the Utah sky. In his memory he saw once again the mirror-like waters of the lake and the way the leaves of the quaking aspen looked like gold and copper pennies in the fall.

If only they had not already paid for tonight's motel—

Or did that even matter? He sat up straight and toyed with the keys in the ignition.

"Help!" Shawn was shouting in a pseudofemale voice as he maneuvered Princess Leia in a leap from the dashboard down onto the open lid of the glove compartment. "Don't worry—I'm coming!" he cried out, his voice now two or three octaves deeper.

"Hey, Luke Skywalker, or whatever your name is, I've got a plan. How about spending the night up at a fabulous lake where Dad used to go a long, long time ago?"

At first Shawn ignored him, making little exploding and whistling sounds with his mouth as he toppled some of the figures out of the glove compartment onto the floor. Then he looked up.

"Go where? To a lake? To sleep? But we don't have anything to—"

"Maybe we could get a cabin or something. They might even have a lodge up there by now for all I know. But what do you say? Okay?"

"What would we sleep in?"

"Hey, don't worry. We can go back down and get your jammies and our toothbrushes and whatever—it's not even five o'clock yet. Are you game?"

Shawn shrugged and smiled broadly. "Whatever you say. You're the boss."

"Then hang on, friend. We're going to zip through space down to the motel and pack up for a place that's truly another world. Ready?"

Again Shawn shrugged. "Whatever!" he said and grinned.

Nine

It was almost dusk when they arrived at the lake. The
sun, through the trees, looked like a giant roasted marsh-
mallow that had caught fire. Even the sky itself began to
seem ablaze overhead, while below, as if lighted by falling
sparks, the once cool, calm expanse of the lake began to
glow with the same fiery intensity.

They found a little cabin to rent, surrounded by quaking aspen, and while the rosy sky faded into a luminous
blue dotted by two or three lone stars, they wandered
among the smoky bonfires along the shore of the lake, listening for a familiar voice, searching in the dusky light
and campfire glow for a familiar face or shape.

Though there seemed to be only one or two general
camping areas, these sprawled endlessly through the trees
and stretched for a long way along the rugged lakeshore. It
was silly, Gavin realized, to try to find anyone in the dark;
they had waited too long and now would have to wait
until morning.

But just as they stood by the still water listening to the
plop followed by the whisperlike ripplings of a fish that
had jumped, they heard, above the faraway hollow sound

of someone chopping wood, a voice say, "Mom, it's that guy and his son—down by the water!"

He turned and peered through the twilight to where a boy in a light shirt hurriedly made his way toward a tent and campfire. There, crouching by the fire, her face and long, pale hair illuminated by the pink-orange glow, was Zin Stokes. She seemed to be stirring something, but they saw her hold up one hand as if to ward off the smoke or maybe to block off the glare of the fire so that she could see better into the darkness beyond.

"Come, Shawn," he whispered, placing his palm against the boy's back and pushing him gently in the direction of the campfire. Zin had stood up now beside Scott and seemed to be watching their approach. He felt a little pang of nervousness: what were they thinking? Would they be disappointed that their little campout was being interrupted by—

"You decided to come, then," Zin's voice broke through the darkness. He thought he could detect a slight smile as well as surprise in her illuminated expression.

"That's right," he returned, as they came up to the fire. "It just sounded too good to pass up."

She was smiling, he saw now, though perhaps more out of mere politeness than genuine pleasure. "Have you already eaten?" she asked.

"Not really, but don't—"

"We don't have much—I'm cooking up a few potatoes and onions—but you're welcome to join."

"I'll tell you what we did," he offered. "We stopped by a supermarket and picked up a bunch of things. Let us share what we have and—"

"We bought some Canadian bacon!" Shawn put in.

"All *right!*" Scott piped up.

"It—it sounds great," Zin said, wiping her hands on the sides of her jeans as she stood up. For a moment she seemed to stand awkwardly as if she were not sure what the next move should be.

"I'll go get everything, okay?" Gavin offered.

"Fine," she said, and her smile, it seemed to him, was reassuring even though her expression still carried the faint look of someone caught suddenly off-guard. "Are you—camping up here?"

"We've got a cabin," he explained. "And we're parked just a little ways up here on the other side of the bend."

"Then take the flashlight," she offered, quickly searching among some things near the fire and then handing it to Shawn.

Gavin looked back at her across the fire, unable to explain even to himself the strange mixture of enthusiasm, embarrassment, even bewilderment, tumbling around inside him. This time she didn't avert her eyes, but returned a gaze that, although he couldn't quite be sure, seemed filled with echoes of the same ambiguities.

Later, after they had finished the last of the eggs, bacon, and potatoes, and consumed most of the black-forest cake brought from the supermarket, the boys took torches from the fire and went down to the edge of the lake, and he found himself alone with Zin as they sat by the glowing coals. For a moment neither of them spoke, then he heard his own voice, even before he had entirely thought through what he wanted to say, cutting into the silence of the night-filled woods.

"I'm glad," he began, "that—that this all worked out. Ever since I saw you last night I knew that there were some things that I ought—that I had to say." He looked at her, but when she returned only the same steady gaze and didn't speak, he went on. "You see, this whole trip out here—out West—is a kind of cleansing for me. I was baptized, by the way—did you know that? I wasn't a member of the Church when we lived out here, but I joined, three or four years later, while I was in the army in Fort Benning, Georgia. That's when I met my wife, Lois, and we were later married in the temple in Washington, D. C. But I guess what I wanted to say was that coming out here has become a kind of a—a second baptism, I guess. I mean, it's been a deliberate attempt to shed a bunch of old memories—memories that have haunted me and, well, made me uncomfortable, I guess you might say."

He looked down at the coals, then back at the strange blue of her eyes, then went on: "Anyway, I wanted to clear up a few things. Some money I owed, a job I never finished—a few little things like that. Nothing major, I guess, although I wanted to try to make things right with J. D. Sargent and maybe try to smooth things over a little since, when I left, we weren't exactly on the best of terms. And then—"

"And Bryce Gunderson?" she asked.

"And Bryce—yeah. I guess I felt I should do something there, although, to tell you the truth, I dreaded that. I think I actually hated that guy. Did you know him very well? I mean, you lived next door to him, or was it after he died that you moved there?"

"My family used to live on a farm," she said, picking up a little stick and poking idly at the coals. "When you were here we lived way out of town, towards Enoch."

"I remember that," he cut in. "In fact, I've never forgotten that night you were in the student council room—remember?" *Well, almost never forgotten. It's true I didn't think about it for thirteen years, but the fact that it was still back there somewhere in my mind must mean something surely* . . . "You had stayed for a meeting that got cancelled or something, and you were telephoning home for a ride."

"I'm surprised you remember that. *I* remember it, of course, but I never thought you would. I was embarrassed—because you came in and caught me crying."

"Now I'm the one that feels bad. I really should have given you a ride home, I guess. Although I can't remember whether I even had my dad's car or whether I had gone up there on my bike." *Or whether I would have just been too ashamed to risk being seen with poor, backward little Zinnie Stokes . . .*

"It was all right. My dad finally came."

"I wish I had taken you home, though. I feel bad about that." He picked up a thin stick and drew little marks in the dirt, steeling himself for what he felt he had to say. "That brings up something else." He glanced over at her, watching her as she went on staring at the dying fire and poking at the last few glowing coals. "I feel like I should clear something up about the Preference Ball."

He saw her rock back, just a little, turning her head away and waving one hand as though the smoke had suddenly drifted her way. But she didn't say anything.

"I was a fool back then," he went on. "I hope you'll forgive me. I—"

"*I* was the fool," he heard her cut in, her voice soft yet husky at the same time. "I should have known you would never have wanted to go with me. In fact, I can hardly believe I ever got up the nerve to ask you. Why on earth I ever thought—"

"Oh, no," he said, trying to cut in, but she made a little motion with her hand for him to let her finish.

"No," she went on. "It was my fault. I had no business asking someone like you to a dance like that—or a dance of any kind. I'm embarrassed to even think—"

"Please," he broke in. "Please don't say that. I should have gone." He looked away, groping for a reason for his action, but, finding nothing he could express, turned back to look at her averted gaze and then the fire. "The least I could have done was to let you know sooner that—" He faltered, realizing that her eyes were now on him.

"Tell me one thing—please," she said. "But don't lie to me." She seemed to swallow, then went on. "I know it was wrong of me to ask you, but I—I did it. And when you never answered—I mean, you could have called or left a note or something . . ."

He felt the old aching starting up inside. Why was it she had remembered so well? How he had wished that the memory was only his and that she had long ago forgotten his little cruelty. "I know what you're saying," he volunteered, "and I apologize for that."

"But just tell me one thing," she repeated. "Was it really that you already had a date, or was it that you just couldn't bear—" She stopped, and he could see that it was very hard for her.

"It wasn't that at all," he began. *It wasn't? Is this your way to make amends? By covering one lie with another, thirteen years later?* He looked down, then back at her. "Actually," he began, "actually I guess I didn't know quite what to do. I guess it came as a sort of a shock. I really didn't know you—"

"And you were embarrassed?"

Embarrassed, yes—yes, I was embarrassed. But how do you say that? And do you even need to say it? "Not really embarrassed—just sort of shocked, I guess. I didn't know you very well."

"And I wasn't really someone that you would have wanted to be seen with," she went on for him. "I knew I didn't have clothes like other girls, and I was plain and didn't know how to fix my hair—"

"Please," he said.

But she went on: "It was my fault. I put you in a diffi-cult position, I know that. I'm embarrassed now to even think that—"

"Look," he said, swallowing. "I was cruel. A lot of us were cruel in those days. But I'm asking you now to forgive me. I saw you the other night, or was it only last night? Yes, it was just last night: I saw you and my heart ached. We were mean, back then, all of us. I look at you now and—honestly—I find you—so—so pretty—and I wonder what was wrong with all of us all those years that we couldn't see that."

"It wasn't your fault," she said, looking embarrassed. "I was a funny little girl. I know that now."

"But it *was* our fault. No one has a right to treat other people the way we treated you. I tried not to be one of them—I honestly did."

"I know you did," she said quietly. "And I think it was your kindness that made me think—that made me feel that maybe, for once, I would dare—"

"And I acted like a fool," he said. He dug forcefully at the ground with the point of his stick. "No, Zin, I didn't have a date at the time you asked me. But I guess I was just too shocked to respond very civilly. You have to remember that I was pretty crazy back then—about someone else." He looked up. "Sharilyn Tebbs. I guess we all were. And don't ask me what it was that seemed to make her so spe-cial."

"Why not? She was pretty, she dressed well, she knew how to fix her hair, and how to act around people. She de-served the popularity. She was talented, outgoing—"

"And each of us hoped she was going to choose us," he said, trying to come up with a little laugh. "And she ended up, I guess, marrying that very guy she took to the dance— the ball-player from St. George—isn't that what you said?"

"I don't remember who she took to the dance," she said, the huskiness back in her voice. "I didn't go, remember?" She glanced away, and seemed to try to smile as she went on, "But I do know that she married a guy named Royden Anderson, and I heard later that they divorced, although——"

"Divorced?" Why was it that the mention of Sharilyn, unmarried, even now seemed to rouse something momentarily inside him?

"I had heard that several years ago, but I think it was probably only a separation, because someone told me not too long ago that they had gotten back together."

He stared into the coals. *If I see you hanging around Sharilyn Tebbs one more time, I'm going to smash your face in:* Bryce Gunderson's mean scowl was there once again rising up before him.

"You know," he found himself saying aloud, "I liked her a lot back then. I think J. D. did, too. But I started taking her out, way back when we were sophomores, and I remember one night Bryce Gunderson threatening me on the steps of the school, telling me that if I ever went near her again he'd beat me to a pulp."

"And did he?"

"No, but I never went with her that much after that either," he laughed. "Not because I was a coward. At least I don't think that was it—not all of it anyway. I think it was mainly because I just couldn't ever feel quite the same about her after that. I mean, anyone who had anything to do with someone like Bryce——"

"And I thought you were here to bury hatchets," she said softly.

"I know," he sighed. "I guess I've still got a long ways to go." He looked into the tiny, flickering flames left in the fire. "I have to admit I did like her. But I wanted some kind of proof that out of all the guys who liked her she had chosen me. And—well—she never did that." He tried to laugh. "That's life, I guess."

"You sound like you're still—still carrying a torch," she said quietly.

"No," he said. "No, not really. That's all over, long ago. When I left here, I pretty well cut myself off from all that. Even from close friends, like J. D., unfortunately. But things just worked out that way," he sighed. "Sometimes it feels almost like I've had two different lives."

She smiled a little bit. "Sometimes I feel like that too."

I'll bet you really do, he thought, looking at the way the soft glow from the coals and an occasional flicker from a flame picked up a sheen in the smooth straight fall of her blond hair. She truly seemed like two different people, and he longed to know when the change had come about and what had made it. He wanted to know how she had felt back in those days when the kids had jeered at her, calling her names and pulling at her braids. He wanted to know how much she had ever dated and whether the father of her child had been someone she had really loved. Why had she never married?

He saw her draw her knees up now under her chin and encircle them with her arms, looking off into the fire, and it occurred to him that he had probably been staring at her for several seconds. But before he could recall what they had just been talking about, it was Zin who broke the silence.

"Tell me—about your wife," she said, her voice almost a whisper.

"My wife," he began, keeping his own voice low as a picture of Lois floated into his consciousness. Funny, he thought, how it was exactly that: a picture, a memory of an actual photograph he kept on the dresser. Why was it so difficult now to remember her in different poses, to picture her from different angles? Why had the photograph become almost more real than the actual woman he had loved so much?

"She was great," he went on. "Lois Dixon—a little Mormon gal from Georgia." He could see her sitting in the Sunday-school class that first day; he could still see the navy-blue dress with the white collar and cuffs, and he could see her hair and how she wore it then, and he could almost see her face—although it was really the face of the photograph, he realized, superimposed on the figure in the church.

"She was quite short, dark, a lot like Shawn, really. A very kind person—optimistic, practical, devoted—what can I say?" For a moment he saw her at their apartment in Cleveland, kissing him good-bye and brushing something off the lapel of his coat.

He looked now at Zin, her chin resting on her clasped hands. He wanted to ask her about Scott's father and wished that she might volunteer something on her own, but she sat quietly, her eyes reflecting the few flames that darted across a log.

Zinnie, Zinnie, tall and skinny . . . What had happened to the odd, backward, and frightened little girl in the hand-me-down clothes? It almost didn't matter; she was gone now, and the lovely, poised woman sitting there by the fire was someone else. He wanted to tell others about her; he longed to see J. D. again and say, *Remember little Zinnie Stokes from out in the valley? You wouldn't believe*— But then he remembered that only he had been away, that J. D. and the others had probably been right here in Cedar City, watching the ugly duckling gradually turn into a swan. He felt cheated now, not knowing what they knew—about her transformation, about her having the child . . . Which came first? he suddenly wondered; he hadn't thought about that. He remembered the tall, unattractive girl in their neighborhood who had had a child out of wedlock when he was still in elementary school. The shame of it all had had no ennobling effects on her that he could recall; in fact, she had seemed to shrivel, grow more sullen, more dejected.

Zinnie Stokes, chews and smokes, Gets her kicks from old cowpokes . . . The words made him cringe. Had they doomed her to that? Had a schoolyard full of mocking children helped to cut out the pattern that a straggly little wallflower was eventually made to follow?

"A penny for your thoughts," came her voice, husky and low. "That's what my mother always used to say."

"My thoughts . . ." he began. "What *are* my thoughts?" *Yes, what are they?* Things he could never say, at least not yet. It was all too soon, so soon it made his head swim, and it was too odd, too bizarre. No matter how he described it, it made no sense: he was sitting here by a smouldering campfire at Navajo Lake with the funny little awkward girl that no one had seemed to like; even when he thought of her as the pale little teenager with the strange haircut and the red eyes and smeared mascara, it was still equally incomprehensible. And when he pictured her as the lonely farm girl who had had an illegitimate child, it puzzled him even more. He could never have planned this moment or even foreseen it. But yet he was here, and not just merely here, but looking across the smoky fire at her with a sympathy and respect—even love? could he actually call it love?—that he had never anticipated, even imagined.

"I didn't mean to stir up sad memories about your wife," he heard her say. "I'm sorry. Forgive me."

My wife . . . Guilt began to gnaw at him, and he noticed that the smoke coming from the coals had grown thicker, heavier. He heard Shawn and Scott laughing and calling out as they ran stumbling toward them, and he was glad for the interruption.

"Dad, can I sleep in the tent with Scott?"

"No, I'm afraid not. Our cabin's waiting for us."

"Then can he come up there? We could put his sleeping bag on the floor, couldn't we?"

"Not tonight. He needs to be here to protect his mother, huh, Scott?" He looked over at Zin who had stood up and was brushing off her jeans. "I feel guilty about us sleeping up there in that cabin while you two are down here in this tent," he said.

"Oh, no," she said, "we love it. Roughing it is part of the fun, isn't it, Scotty?"

"Can we all go on a canoe ride, then? Early in the morning?" Shawn begged.

"Sure!" he shrugged. "Why not?" He glanced at Zin for approval.

Zinnie, Zinnie, his mind began reciting; and the rhyme went on even as he told her goodnight and they made their way through the dark up to the cabin in the trees. *Zinnie Stokes, chews and smokes,* he forced himself to mentally recite, sensing that the old incantation might be necessary to ward off the strange new feelings he was not yet quite ready to accept.

Ten

The lake, in the early morning, was remarkably like glass as they pushed away from the dock and listened to the paddles slipping almost silently into its clear coolness. Shawn and Scott had been laughing as they bounded down through the trees and made their way to the little cabin on the shore marked BOAT RENTALS; but once they climbed into the canoe and pushed off onto the mirrorlike stillness of the lake, the laughter grew momentarily hushed, and they all sat motionless as if in awe of something so pristine, so unspoiled.

Gavin dipped in the paddle, first on one side and then on the other, and then paused, letting their canoe drift noiselessly while the prow sent silver diagonals rippling back as it cut through the glassy water. The already spectacular panorama of trees, mountains, and sky that wrapped around them repeated itself upside-down with uncanny perfection in the smooth surface of the lake.

"It's like we're floating through space," Shawn quietly breathed, his neck withdrawn turtlelike into the stiff shell of his shoulders while he perched gingerly on the narrow seat, his hands poised, as if in fearful readiness, on each side of the canoe.

Gavin watched Zin as she pushed back the hair from the sides of her face and looked across the lake, her eyes, alert and vibrant, seeming to drink in the radiance of the early morning. Once again he was struck by the rightness of it all, by the way her eyes and hair and skin seemed to be a part of the lake and the quaking aspen and the crisp fresh air.

"This is my favorite time of day," she said, smiling, still looking off across the still, clear water. "Even my favorite time of the year."

He smiled back. "It suits you." He let the tip of the oar slip silently into the lake's surface with scarcely a ripple.

Occasionally a bird flew overhead; across the lake behind them, a wisp of smoke from a morning campfire lazily spiraled up through the trees; before them, where the water had risen high enough this year to move the shoreline into the aspen, the clean white bark of the trees emerged from its own reflection and disappeared in the tiny circles of fresh leaves that waited for a breeze to make them flutter and shiver silver-green in the early sunlight.

"Mom, could we get out and play over on this side of the lake for a while?" Scott asked, his eyes busily scanning the approaching shore.

"Yeah!" Shawn seconded. "It would be great for playing Indians!"

The boat drifted closer to where the submerged aspen rose up from the silver mirror of the lake. Carefully Gavin maneuvered the canoe so that it slid easily between the trees, and for a few hushed moments they slipped through the maze of slim white trunks running parallel with the shoreline.

"What about it? Should we let them run wild for a while over here?" he asked.

Zin smiled and shrugged.

"Do all your exploring around in here somewhere," he advised, "and we'll come back by in about twenty minutes or half an hour—okay?"

"Great!" the boys yelled, and he used the paddle gondolier-style to push them closer to the shore so the boys could step out onto the rocks and climb up the hillside.

"They get along amazingly well considering the age difference," he said, watching them disappear into the greenery. "How old did you say Scott is?"

"Eleven," she said. "But he missed never having a brother." Then a tinge of color seemed to come into her face, and she turned partly away, pushing back some of the long strands of silver-gold hair from her cheek.

"All I can say is, you've done amazingly well with him," he said. Then, on an impulse, he decided to barrel forward. "I guess you—pretty much raised him all by yourself."

Again he sensed that her cheeks seemed to take on more color, but she gave her head a little shake as if to compose herself as well as to free her hair from her neck and shoulders.

"Pretty much," she said quietly, maintaining a little smile. "Grandparents, of course, help out a lot. My dad loved Scotty and used to take him along to feed the horses or fix the fence or whatever. But his health hasn't been good. He has emphysema, and after my mother died, he decided to sell the ranch and live with my sister in Arizona."

"He's pretty lucky—Scott, I mean—to have a mother that will go camping with him in the mountains. I think you're probably a better father to him than I am a mother to Shawn."

She smiled and let one hand dip lightly into the water as the canoe continued to drift slowly in and out of the

She opened her mouth to speak, yet looked away. "It—it isn't that. It's just that—I have—obligations."

He wanted to turn away, but instead he swallowed and pursued the question further: "Obligations?"

She pulled a tiny new branch of soft green pine needles from the trunk of a tree and absentmindedly pulled it apart. "Nothing really all that important, I guess." She looked up. "All right. Maybe we can get together later on this evening, or maybe tomorrow . . ."

"How about this evening? Would that work okay?"

She took another deep breath. "I think so. I—"

"But where'll I find you?"

She crumpled the remaining soft needles in her hands and, shredding them between her palms, let them drop. "Maybe at the little house. I should be there later on. Would that be all right?"

"Your place? Where you used to live?"

She nodded.

"What time?"

"Maybe—maybe about eight-thirty. Or nine?"

"Great. I'll see you between eight-thirty and nine. Okay?"

"Okay."

He smiled at her and saw her smile timidly back before her eyes looked away. He wanted to reach out and touch her hair or her cheek, but she made a motion to go, and together they made their way down the mountainside, hearing the sounds of their boys from far away mingling with the hollow rat-a-tat of a woodpecker and the distant muffled chopping of wood.

It was not until they came around the last turn and started the descent directly into the valley that Gavin remembered the appointment with Mrs. Mendenhall. He

trees. "It's hard," she said. "But we do what
I guess."

For almost an hour they talked, the canc
under the leafy aspen while the sun shim
open part of the lake. Twice the boys begged
to hike in the hills and climb in the brancl
they consented while they lounged in the
canoe under the shade of the trees. They tall
of his work, of her job in Logan, of raising bc
about books and movies, of some poetry sl
write, and many other things he could
member as they started back, the four of tl
slowly toward the other shore. He wanted tl
the morning to last forever. But by mid-day,
shared a sausage-and-pancake breakfast
short hike up into the pines, he could sense
was imminent.

The light filtered down through the pi
pling her hair and shoulders with silver-gol
saw her glance at her watch, and then he
blue haze, met his.

"I guess I need to think about going bε
"There are some things I need to do in towr

"When do you have to go back to Logan

"Day after tomorrow."

The words jarred him. Two more days
one, depending on what time she would
Saturday. He wanted more time, needed m

"So when do I see you again?"

Her eyes rested for a moment on his, bu
tect no change in her expression. Then she sl
and took a deep breath. "I—I really don't l
quite a lot I have to do."

He was beginning to feel hurt, even bru
it? Don't you want to see me again?"

trees. "It's hard," she said. "But we do what we have to do, I guess."

For almost an hour they talked, the canoe meandering under the leafy aspen while the sun shimmered on the open part of the lake. Twice the boys begged for more time to hike in the hills and climb in the branches, and twice they consented while they lounged in the gently rocking canoe under the shade of the trees. They talked of the East, of his work, of her job in Logan, of raising boys; they talked about books and movies, of some poetry she had tried to write, and many other things he couldn't totally remember as they started back, the four of them, paddling slowly toward the other shore. He wanted the day to go on, the morning to last forever. But by mid-day, after they had shared a sausage-and-pancake breakfast and taken a short hike up into the pines, he could sense that a parting was imminent.

The light filtered down through the pine trees, dappling her hair and shoulders with silver-gold patterns. He saw her glance at her watch, and then her eyes, soft as blue haze, met his.

"I guess I need to think about going back," she said. "There are some things I need to do in town today."

"When do you have to go back to Logan?"

"Day after tomorrow."

The words jarred him. Two more days—maybe only one, depending on what time she would be leaving on Saturday. He wanted more time, needed more time.

"So when do I see you again?"

Her eyes rested for a moment on his, but he could detect no change in her expression. Then she shifted her eyes and took a deep breath. "I—I really don't know. There's quite a lot I have to do."

He was beginning to feel hurt, even bruised. "What is it? Don't you want to see me again?"

She opened her mouth to speak, yet looked away. "It—it isn't that. It's just that—I have—obligations."

He wanted to turn away, but instead he swallowed and pursued the question further: "Obligations?"

She pulled a tiny new branch of soft green pine needles from the trunk of a tree and absentmindedly pulled it apart. "Nothing really all that important, I guess." She looked up. "All right. Maybe we can get together later on this evening, or maybe tomorrow . . ."

"How about this evening? Would that work okay?"

She took another deep breath. "I think so. I—"

"But where'll I find you?"

She crumpled the remaining soft needles in her hands and, shredding them between her palms, let them drop. "Maybe at the little house. I should be there later on. Would that be all right?"

"Your place? Where you used to live?"

She nodded.

"What time?"

"Maybe—maybe about eight-thirty. Or nine?"

"Great. I'll see you between eight-thirty and nine. Okay?"

"Okay."

He smiled at her and saw her smile timidly back before her eyes looked away. He wanted to reach out and touch her hair or her cheek, but she made a motion to go, and together they made their way down the mountainside, hearing the sounds of their boys from far away mingling with the hollow rat-a-tat of a woodpecker and the distant muffled chopping of wood.

It was not until they came around the last turn and started the descent directly into the valley that Gavin remembered the appointment with Mrs. Mendenhall. He groaned aloud, feeling a need to share his blunder with someone, but Shawn was still asleep on the back seat.

"What a fool!" he went on moaning to himself anyway. "I wait fifteen or sixteen years to make something right, and then I bumble it up again."

They *had* set it up for this morning, hadn't they? Again he groaned, thinking of the shriveled little lady pacing the floor and peeking out through the curtains every few minutes, wondering why they hadn't come.

He drove directly to her house, his head brimming with apologies. Three times he knocked on the door before she answered it.

"Mrs. Mendenhall," he began, as soon as she opened the door a little and peeked through the crack. "I'm sorry we didn't come this morning—"

"Didn't what?" she asked, opening the door a little wider and turning her ear toward the opening.

"I'm sorry," he began again, louder, "but my son and I were supposed to come this morning and clean up your basement."

She looked puzzled, then, steadying one trembling hand against her cheek, blinked at him and shook her head back and forth slowly. "Oh, dear me. I think I forgot completely." She made an effort to scoot herself part way around, then turned back. "It was today, was it?"

He felt his body relax with relief. *No, not today— tomorrow*, he wanted to say, but the words were already starting to come out: "It was supposed to be today—but I took my boy up to Navajo Lake and didn't get ba—"

"Took him where? Where is he? You didn't leave him there, did you?" She suddenly seemed very alert.

"No, no, he's in the car, asleep. We've had a long day. But we'd like to come tomorrow morning, if that's all right."

She smiled again and, holding up one of her hands, let

it flutter a minute near the side of her head before she spoke. "Of course it's all right. You're the boy who never finished your job, aren't you?" She chuckled, apparently pleased with the memory. "You'll come. I know you will." She was already scooting sideways as if it were all settled and she were about to close the door.

"Tomorrow morning, then—okay?" he asked, pronouncing the words carefully.

"Tomorrow morning," he heard her mumble. Then, another chuckle, "I'll try to be ready for you." And he thought he saw her head bobbing in amusement as she closed the door softly and turned away.

He spent part of the afternoon running little errands— filling the car with gas, picking up some light globes for Mrs. Mendenhall's basement, checking J. D.'s St. George address in the telephone directory, taking a potted plant to Mrs. Bigelow—then he took a nap at the motel while Shawn played *Star Wars* on the rungs of the chair and under the little writing table.

When he awoke, he showered and shaved, surprising himself by singing under the steaming water and in front of the mirror with a boyish vigor he hadn't felt in years. Then the two of them ate cheeseburgers and french fries while he watched the clock tick its way toward eight o'clock. He talked briefly with a few old-timers on the street, then they strolled down Main Street, lingering in front of the windows of the closed shops until it was nearly eight-thirty.

By eight-forty they were pulling up in front of the little stone house with the hollyhocks. Once again it surprised him that the front yard was still full of weeds; but what surprised him more was that the house looked dark even though the dusky twilight seemed to be settling quickly over the neighborhood. A little breeze had come up, and it seemed as though part of the oncoming darkness might be due to storm clouds gathering overhead.

"Come on, let's give it a try," he mumbled to Shawn as they left the car and passed through the little gate. But he could feel the emptiness, the disappointment, encroaching upon him.

It was true. No one was there. He hesitated uneasily on the doorstep, knocking briskly, waiting, then knocking one last time. Was it simply that they were too early? Or was it just that her other plans had detained her a little longer than she had anticipated? He shifted his weight, looked restlessly at the houses nearby, their lights glowing, and glanced once more at his watch.

Then he looked up. A screen door banged somewhere nearby, and he saw, in the fading light, someone hurrying along the sidewalk between the picket fence and the road.

It was Zin, her hair pulled back and fastened someway behind. She was carrying something in her hand that he couldn't quite make out. Then he saw it was an old-fashioned coal-oil lamp, unlighted.

"I'm sorry," she was saying. "I thought I'd be here before you arrived." She seemed out of breath. "I just borrowed a lamp from next door. I forgot there'd be no lights on in here."

"Where's Scott?" Shawn asked.

"Next door," she answered, handing Gavin the lamp while she fumbled in her pocket for a key to the front door. "He's putting a jigsaw puzzle together and would love to have you help him. If you want to come with me, I'll walk you over there."

She unlocked the door, fumbled again in her pocket, this time for matches, and seemed nervous as she set the lamp on the table and lighted it.

"Just sit down here a minute," she said to Gavin. "In

fact, you could make a little fire in the fireplace, if you want. It feels almost cool enough tonight." She knelt at the fireplace, removed the cardboard propped in front of it, and worked the damper back and forth. "I think that's open now. There's still some wood here—and here are the matches."

She stood up, brushing off her hands, and looked at Shawn. "Want to come with me? Scott's watching TV and working on a gigantic thousand-piece puzzle."

Shawn shrugged and smiled, glancing questioningly over at Gavin, then took her hand and started with her out of the house.

"I'll be right back," she said, still seeming a little out of breath. And then she stepped out into the darkness, letting the screen door close softly behind them.

For a moment he stood awkwardly in the middle of the little room. The yellowish light from the lamp cast shadows that seemed to bring the walls and the ceiling in even closer to him, and he realized how Alice in Wonderland must have felt when she ate the little piece of cake that made her suddenly increase in size. He walked to the screen door and looked out just as Zin and Shawn disappeared through the gate and into the night. Above, the sky looked heavy and dark as though the indigo clouds were sodden with a thick, blue-black ink. From the distant hills where the sky touched down in a dusky yet luminous blue, came a long, low rumble of thunder.

He set about making the fire, finding enough newspaper and kindling wood to get it started. It had just burst into a crackling blaze when a flash of lightning starkly illuminated the room for a second, followed by a resounding crash of thunder. He could hear her footsteps running up the walk, then the first rattling sound, like gravel sprinkled on a tin roof, that signaled the beginning of the downpour. He leaped up to throw open the screen door for her, and as she ran in, her hands covering her head, she almost fell into his arms.

He held her there for a moment, smelling the fresh, almost piney, scent of her hair, his hand on the back of her head bringing her cheek in against his neck and chest. She was breathing deeply, and he could feel the rhythm of their heartbeats. He kissed the silkiness of her hair once lightly, then he kissed it again.

He could feel the palms of her hands move up against his chest, and then he felt her gently push away. The eyes, pale blue and searching, looked into his.

"Gavin," she whispered. "Please. I've got to tell you something."

His eyes were searching hers now. What was she about to say? He remembered once again the gawky and ungainly girl—Elva? Elma?— who had lived in their neighborhood almost twenty years ago, and he remembered how, a year or two after her illegitimate child was born, one of the single male schoolteachers had taken her somewhere. He could still hear Mrs. Bigelow's voice as she halfwhispered to his mother on the front porch, "I don't think he ought to be doing that. People will talk."

He reached out one hand and touched Zin's cheek. Then he leaned forward and kissed her lightly on the forehead. Whatever she had done in the past, he forgave her. He wanted to defend her, protect her. He wanted—

She pulled away once more. "Please," she said. "Don't you know who I am?"

What was she talking about? *Zinnie, Zinnie, tall and skinny* . . . If he was willing to forget all of that, why wasn't she? Didn't she realize he wanted to put all of that behind them? For him, the awkward little farm girl was long gone. Even the girl who had given her heart to a stranger and had had his child. He forgave her for that; it was over, gone. It didn't matter anymore.

"Tell me my name, Gavin," she whispered huskily. "Please say it."

Zinnie Stokes, chews and smokes... What was she forcing him to do? And why? Was she bringing all that up to punish him? To remind him of all the pain and humiliation she had suffered in those awful years? Why—

"Tell me who I am," she said softly, looking down. "I want to hear you say it."

He paused. He would not say *Zinnie*. He wouldn't even say *Zinnia*. She had introduced herself as Zin, and he would call her that—forever.

"You're Zin Stokes," he said, his own voice sounding hoarse and foreign to him.

She shook her head. "No, Gavin. Not Zin Stokes. I'm Zin Gunderson."

Eleven

For a few seconds he was aware only of the rain falling heavily upon the roof. The fire flickered, casting strange shadows around them.

"What are you saying?" he managed.

She put her palms lightly on his chest and looked away as if trying to catch her breath. Then she took her hands down and clasped them nervously. But her eyes found his and fastened on his gaze. "I'm Zin Gunderson, Bryce's wife."

"Bryce? What are talking about? You told me Bryce died a year or so after I left! Are you trying to tell me Scott is—"

"He's Bryce's son—our son, mine and Bryce's—but Bryce never saw him. He was killed two months before Scotty was born."

The rain was too loud. It was becoming hard to hear, hard to even think. He reached out with his hand and pushed the door shut, cutting out some of the noise. He was aware now of the angry popping and crackling of the fire.

"Wait a minute," he said. "I don't get this at all." He

reached out and took her left hand, rubbing his fingers over hers. "Why no ring? Why did you tell me yourself, out by the garden, that you were Zin Stokes?" The loudness of his voice surprised him, but it seemed almost beyond his control.

She withdrew her hand, then leaned back against the closed door, her hands behind her. "I know it's my fault. I said Zin Stokes because I knew that was the name you would know me by—if you remembered me at all."

"But why—"

She went on: "And the ring. No, I don't have a ring. I haven't had a ring for almost ten years." She looked down, then back at him. "But there *was* a ring. Not when we first got married—but a few days later. Bryce's mother gave it to me. It was hers, but she couldn't wear it anymore because of her arthritis. But I lost it a long time ago." She blushed and found some sort of an embarrassed smile: "I lost it years ago, bottling apricots."

His stomach felt knotted, and the steady sound of rain on the roof made his head hurt. "I don't get it," he said. "I don't understand why you never said—"

"How could I?" she asked. "From the moment you came up to me out by the garden, you told me how much you despised him."

He cringed. "I'm sorry," he managed to say.

She seemed about to say something but then stopped.

"I wish I had known," he said, feeling empty, embarrassed. "I made a fool of myself."

"I'm sorry, too," she said, "for not telling you. After you told me your feelings about him—the other night out by the fence—I was glad I hadn't told you anything. And I saw no point—in—in embarrassing you." She hesitated. "I thought, when you left, that it really didn't matter— because I didn't expect to ever see you again."

"I should have known there was something," he said

quietly, letting himself down onto a chair. "When you told me you lived here, and then I came and—"

"Again, I'm sorry," she said. "I never meant to lie to you. We did live here, Bryce and I, right after we were married. And I lived here by myself after he went into the army. I went on living here, in fact, with Scott until he was about three." She moved away from the door and stood by the table staring at the lamp. "Gundersons own it. They built it for the grandfather years ago, and then he died. They fixed it up for Bryce and me, and we—we lived here—for a little while."

She turned the lamp down just a little. The fire flickered, changing the patterns of light and shadow around the room. He wanted to say something but couldn't think of what it was. He only knew that his head hurt and he wanted the rain to let up.

"Do you remember—how I was?"

"How you—?"

"How I was back in those days when you knew me," she went on. "I was so shy—and I hated myself. You remember, I guess, how the kids all used to make fun of me." She took a deep breath and began walking nervously around the room. He motioned for her to sit down, but she gave her head a little shake and went on, "I hated my name and where we lived and the clothes I had to wear—at least when I was in high school. If you knew, if you only knew how much I wanted to—to be in on things—to be liked. For a long time I told myself it didn't matter, but when I was a junior, I used to—I used to cry a lot about that."

She stood in front of the fireplace, her back toward him, then she turned around. "The year after you left, I tried to fix myself up as best I could. We never had much money for clothes or things like that, but I learned to sew. I wanted to be somebody. I wanted someone to notice me. I wonder if you can imagine what it was like—to never have a date? I never did—not once that I can remember. Not even once."

He tried not to think of the Preference Ball, but the image of her in the hall kept returning: *It's okay.* Her eyes—hurt, embarrassed—trying to look away. *I wasn't really planning on it, anyway . . .*

"I made a real effort, the last of my junior year. My sister cut my hair and I spent everything I had on a certain sweater and a skirt. And I started going to dances—"

"You began dating then?" he interrupted.

"No. There were two girls that lived out my way—the Thompson girls. One of them would drive the pickup and bring us into town. We would go by ourselves and stand on the sidelines. You remember how that was." She paused, then lifted her chin a little and went on. "Sometimes someone asked me to dance, usually someone from out of town. And once or twice that winter they even asked to take me home. But I never went. I didn't know them and I—I was afraid, I guess. The youngest Thompson girl—Rolaine—began going out with a guy from Toquerville, so LaNita and I would just go by ourselves."

She stopped for a moment, taking a long deep breath, then continued: "That spring something strange happened. Bryce had been going with Sharilyn Tebbs, breaking up and then getting back together all winter. But in the spring—at graduation time—she had started going again with the Anderson fellow from St. George. I'm sure Bryce thought he could get her to break it off, but suddenly she shows up at graduation with a diamond—and Bryce is furious. He came to the Graduation Dance, by himself, but he had been drinking. I suppose he did it to punish her. He danced with everyone that night—and near the end of the dance began spending most of the time with me. I can see now what a fool I was, but I was flattered. I knew he was a little drunk, but he said things to me that no one had ever said before—*ever*. I remember how he would stop and look at me in between dances and say things like, 'You know, you're really beautiful. Where have you been hiding all my life?'"

She stopped and swallowed, then, rubbing the palms of her hands together nervously, started again: "I know I was foolish. But the way he put his arm around me and took me out to the car, I felt happier—and more loved— than I had ever felt in my life. I had been having a bad time at home—I had even wanted to run away—and suddenly here was this football player a year older than me telling me he loved me and—and daring me to run away with him and marry him."

She looked as if she were about to cry, but she managed to go on. "We did get married that night, on a whim, in the middle of the night. I guess I must have known even then that he was only doing it to hurt Sharilyn, but I was so desperately in need of being loved, and my head was spinning with all the attention and affection that—some- how—I went along with it. We were married about three- thirty in the morning by a justice of the peace just over the state line in Nevada. I was not even seventeen yet—not for two more months—but we lied about my age."

She started to pace around the room, then she went back to the fireplace and fidgeted with the matches on the mantel. "The next morning," she went on, "we both came to our senses and realized what we had done. I think he wanted an annulment, but it was too late. I knew I had done the wrong thing, but still I felt that if we tried, we could make it work. I was willing to do anything—any- thing. His parents fixed this little place up for us and helped him get a job, but within three days he had joined the army. I didn't see him for six months. In the meantime I had gone back to school to try to finish, even though, by then, I was pregnant with Scotty. In December his mother told me he was coming home on leave, and I was sure that, with the baby coming in February, things would be different. I fixed this place up as nicely as I could, determined to be the best wife and mother I could be—but when he arrived, just before Christmas, he let me know very clearly that he had only come back because he was still in love with Sharilyn and he was going to do all he could to stop her marriage. Two days later, he was killed in a car wreck. He had been drinking again."

Gavin felt the need to get up and go to her. She had turned away from him and stood holding to the mantel, her head lowered as if staring at the fire. He put his arms around her from behind, but there was an awkwardness, a stiffness, that he felt in both of them.

"Scott was born in February," she went on, "and the next year, while his mother tended the baby, I went back to school and graduated. We lived here, Scotty and I, for two more years, then I felt I had to get away. That's when we went to Logan, and I started working there at the university and taking classes. I decided it was up to me to change my life, and I tried to improve my grammar, the way I looked, and—"

"Zin," he said, noting the hoarseness in his voice. "You've made an amazing change."

"I don't cry for myself anymore," he heard her say. "Scotty, my work, good books—these things fulfill me, and I don't ask for anything more."

For a moment they both were silent. There was a perceptible coldness between them, and he let his hands slip from around her waist. Still he couldn't move, and he stood there behind her, close enough that he could smell the scent of pine in her hair.

"Did you love him?" he asked.

"Does it matter?" she asked, turning partly away. "He

hurt me," she said huskily, "but I was willing to try to love him."

Could you learn to love me? he had wanted to ask earlier, but he couldn't say the words now. Something was wrong; something had changed.

The rain still beat down steadily upon the roof, but it was quieter now and more even. The thunder had stopped. In the fireplace an occasional flame flickered, then disappeared.

"You—you'll be leaving day after tomorrow?" he finally managed to ask.

"Yes," she said, her back still toward him.

"Maybe there would be some time tomorrow that we—"

"It might be hard. Mrs. Gunderson is coming home from the hospital. She's been very ill—diabetes. She'll have one of her daughters with her but—"

"Is that where you've been staying? Over at Gundersons'?"

"Yes," she answered softly. "That night you came there, I just happened to be over here pulling a few weeds in case we try to rent the place again."

He glanced at the room, the light from the coal-oil lamp and the last few flames of the fire giving its bare walls and shelves an old-fashioned, even primitive, look, like some early pioneer dwelling. For a moment, he strained to picture the young Zin and Bryce, runaway newlyweds, surrounded by these walls, confronting at last the consequences of what they had done, but it made him uncomfortable, and he quickly tried to shake the image away. He reached out toward her shoulder, wondering if the touch of his hand would cause her to turn finally and face him. But instead she seemed to let her cheek fall lightly against her arms, which rested on the mantel.

"I'll try to catch you sometime tomorrow," he began.

At this she turned to face him. "It would be better—
for me, I think—if we just said our good-byes now. It
would—"

"I don't understand," he heard himself blurting out.

"The past is all tidied up now, isn't it? You've made
your apologies and straightened out all the—"

"Wait a minute," he interrupted. "You sound angry."

"I'm sorry," she said, "because I'm really not—upset. I
just don't want to complicate things." She lowered her
eyes, but before he could speak, she was looking up at him
and trying to go on, "I admire your—your determination
to straighten up the past—but I'm not sure I like what it's
doing to the present."

She started to turn away a little, and he found himself
reaching out to take her arms or her shoulders. Still she
pulled away. "You come back here, digging up old ghosts,
stirring up dead ashes . . ."

"You seem to be blaming me for—"

"I can't help it," she said, crying now. "How can you
meddle with people's lives this way? You come here stirring up feelings that were long ago buried—"

He grabbed her arms. "Slow down a minute," he said,
trying to draw her closer to him, even though she still re-
sisted. "What feelings are you talking about?"

"I don't have them any longer. They're gone!"

Her eyes, clouded with tears, tried to look away, but
for a moment, he forced her to look at him. "What feelings?" he repeated. "Your feelings for Bryce?"

"Please," she said. "Please!"

"I'm sorry, Zin, but *what* feelings? For Bryce?"

"It doesn't matter. They're gone, and I don't want to
stir them up. I can't go through that anymore. I don't need
that."

He loosened his grip on her, but still held her by her

upper arms. "I'm sorry I've upset you. I didn't mean to dig up any painful memories."

"I know it's not your fault," she broke in. "I was just a silly little girl with ridiculous dreams and I had no right to involve you, no right at all. So please, let's not involve each other now."

"What dreams? Tell me," he urged. "How did they involve me?"

"Please go," she said softly. "I'm not even making sense. I can't even think clearly. I just wanted to explain to you about Bryce, and then I wanted you to go."

"If you really want me to go, I won't stay. But I wish you would tell me one thing."

She relaxed a little, staring at him, then took a deep breath. "What is that?"

"Last night," he began, "at least I think it was last night—you asked me to tell you one thing, whether I actually had a date or not when I turned you down for that dance thirteen years ago. I told you—and I told you honestly: no, I did not have a date, at least not when you asked me. I'm sorry for that—it was wrong of me, and I wish I had been big enough to handle it right. But now, you tell *me* something—and tell me honestly: what feelings are these that you claim I'm stirring up?"

She was quiet for a moment. Though her eyes were still moist, there were no tears. She breathed deeply and seemed to be looking into space slightly past his shoulder.

"A long time ago," she finally began, "*years* ago, there was a pathetic little girl named Zinnie Stokes. But I'm not her anymore—believe me, I'm *not* her. But Zinnie Stokes used to think that Gavin Terry was the most wonderful person in the world. Maybe it was because you were the only person that ever treated me kindly at all—I don't really know. I wasn't even sure you knew who I was, but I used to see you in the halls and at the assemblies, and I thought you had the kindest eyes I had ever seen." She stopped for a moment, took a breath, and then began again. "I used to dream—daydream—that one day you would notice me, and then by the look in your eyes, I would somehow know that you loved me and—"

"I think I almost felt like that the night I met you out here by the garden," he broke in softly.

She raised one hand and touched his lips lightly with her fingers. "Let me finish," she whispered. "You gave me no reason, really, to have those feelings, and how I ever got up the courage to ask you to that dance, I'll never know. You turned me down—but you did it kindly. You had your reasons, and believe me, I understand them. I forgave you long ago, Gavin, I honestly did. That was a long, long time ago, and I had almost forgotten you completely." Again she paused. "For several years now, I've been very much in control of my life—of who I am and who I want to be. Please don't make me Zinnie Stokes again."

"What do you mean?"

"I just mean, don't mix up my life. I was a sad and lonely little girl who longed for something she couldn't have. I'm all over that now. You see, life to me then was like one of those trick valentines. When you went to pick them up from the doorstep, someone pulled a string and they disappeared. Please don't—"

"Is that what you think I'm doing to you now?"

"I don't want to think that, no. But things are awfully confused right now for both of us. I had no trouble forgiving you before, Gavin—I really didn't. But I couldn't forgive you so easily now. So please, I've told you some things that can't help but matter. I *am* Zin Gunderson, and although I can tell you honestly that I never really loved Bryce Gunderson—I hardly had a chance to—still, my little Scotty, the dearest thing to me in all the world, is

Bryce's son. That's no valentine with a string on it. That's a fact we both have to accept."

He wanted to speak, but there was something that seemed to be crowding into his chest and throat that wouldn't let him talk. The constant drumming of the rain hurt his head, and the room seemed to be closing in on him from all sides. Before he could find the words he wanted, she spoke again. "Listen, the rain has almost stopped." The idea jolted him until he actually listened and became aware that the throbbing and pounding he had been hearing came from somewhere inside his own head. The patter on the roof was sporadic now, coming in little splatters as though the wind occasionally sent a gust of drops from the nearby trees, scattering them across the roof. "I want you to go now," she went on. "I'll walk over to Gundersons with you to get Shawn, but I want you to go. Our minds are not clear tonight—at least I know mine is not. I want to do some thinking—and praying. And tomorrow—"

"I'll see you tomorrow then?"

"If you want, we'll see each other tomorrow. But maybe late in the day. We need—"

"I'll tell you what," he said. "I'll meet you here just about dusk—just about the time the sun goes down, the way it was the first night when I met you out by the fence."

"All right," she agreed, her voice little more than a whisper. "Meet me there—where you saw me then."

For a moment they looked at each other, then, just as he moved toward her, she raised her fingers to her lips, kissed them lightly and then placed them softly on his own. He felt torn: he wanted to pull her to him, to kiss her hair, her cheeks, her lips, yet there was something inside him aching—like a wound throbbing in the middle of the night when the pain pills have worn away—and the hurt almost wouldn't let him move.

She opened the screen door, letting in the smell of rain on the sidewalk and on the grass and the trees. They both looked back at the fireplace where the last few coals smouldered quietly. She went over and, for a moment, prodded them gently with a poker. Next she went to the lamp and turned it down all the way until the flame was only a tiny flicker. And then she blew it out.

Twelve

Shawn stuck close by his side the next morning as they descended the stairs into Mrs. Mendenhall's basement and screwed in one of the new light bulbs he had bought. The imagined dimensions of the room leaped suddenly to conform to the real walls and boundaries as light instantly illuminated everything around them. The space itself was large and even had two or three dark little pantries and closets leading off from it, yet almost every corner, every shelf, even most of the floor itself appeared to be crowded with boxes and cans, barrels and bottles. And although just the presence of the light seemed enough to calm Shawn's fears so that he began to wander from Gavin's side to poke at a pair of old ice skates or peek into a dusty cigar box, Gavin himself was struck by the thickness of the dust and the abundance of cobwebs now visible.

They rummaged through bird cages and butter churns, washing-machine ringers and chamber pots. They found navy uniforms from World War II and came across boxes of magazines with issues spanning six decades. For most of the morning they searched out the different sections of a collapsible baby crib, sorted usable canning bottles, and took up load after load of candy boxes filled with marbles, buttons, and bolts for Mrs. Mendenhall to sort through.

Shawn seemed thoroughly entranced, but more than once Gavin found himself shifting boxes and thumbing through old books without paying any attention at all to what he was doing. Other images paraded through his mind: a scrawny little girl with bone-white pigtails gazing out of the cloudy window of the schoolbus; a pale girl looking uncomfortable with her new haircut and new sweater as she rides quietly along a winter road in the cab of a pickup that smells of spilled milk and manure; an anemic-looking young girl, seven-months pregnant and burdened by the weight of her new role as wife and mother, trying to do her high-school homework while she watches out of the frosty window for the return of the soldier-husband who abandoned her three days after their marriage.

He tried to picture her, maybe in the heavy jacket and knitted cap of an older brother, milking the cows on a cold January morning; and he tried to imagine her getting off the schoolbus in the dark and stumbling among the ruts as she made her way down a long narrow lane leading to the farmhouse. He saw her learning to drive a tractor, helping to mend a barbed-wire fence, and finally playing quietly with some mangy cats, all by herself, in the dusky loft of an old barn.

There was a gap between them, and he had to acknowledge that. Even though they had grown up in the same general area and gone to the same schools, their lives had been vastly different. He had recognized that clearly as a child: the strange little girl with frightened eyes had always seemed alien, out of place. Why, then, had he deluded himself now into imagining some closeness, some bond? *I had no right to involve you, no right at all. So please, let's not involve each other now.* Was she right, then, after all?

He could see her, more radiantly otherworldly than simply alien, standing in that hushed moment before evening sets in, the deep pink flowers overflowing in her arms; and he saw her against the pine trees and the aspen, her silky hair splashed with sunlight. Yet another image kept nudging at these, pushing them out of the way. It was her, suddenly married to Bryce Gunderson, then awkwardly pregnant with his child, her expression as well as her shoulders drooping wearily under some unseen load. At times he tried to shut it out; at other times he tried to force himself to bring it clearly into focus. Either way it haunted him, irritated him, upset him. Why was it, he kept asking himself as he piled boxes and cleared off shelves in the musty basement, why was it that he had been able to handle more easily the possibility of her having had a baby out of wedlock than the reality of having given birth legitimately to a child of Bryce Gunderson?

"Dad," Shawn was asking, "do you think that grandma lady would still want this?" He held up a battered little lead soldier, crouched ready for battle, its bayonet as well as part of its arm broken off and rusted.

"Probably not—it's pretty beat up. Might as well just stick it in that pile over there."

"But I want it!"

"You'd have to ask her first. But we can't be hauling a bunch of junk home. Look at this stuff!" He picked up an orange crate, dingy with dust, filled with a corroded assortment of broken fixtures and appliances—a waffle iron, a fuel pump, a lamp base.

By the time they finished, they had located all the parts of a quilting frame she had been worrying about, discovered an old stationery box bulging with photographs and faded greeting cards she had long forgotten, and organized everything else as best they could on the rickety shelves. She let them wash up while she heated some rice pudding in a little pan on her stove; then she fed them and thanked them while she poked among the boxes on the couch, wiping her eyes and mumbling to herself.

She kept the little soldier but gave Shawn a stringless ukelele, a plaster-of-paris figurine of the Lone Ranger, a pocketful of marbles, and a stack of dusty Hardy Boy books. By two-thirty in the afternoon, they were saying their good-byes and waving back at her as she peeked out at them through the lace curtains in the door.

"D'you feel better now, Dad?" Shawn asked.

Better? His mind still wandered to the little house a few blocks away where a quiet, sixteen-year-old farm girl had tried painfully to take on the role of Mrs. Bryce Gunderson. But better? Physically, he was tired: his back ached and his neck felt stiff; mentally, he felt drained, exhausted by the confused and conflicting images that had been wrestling in his mind. But better? Yes, he could say that.

"Huh, Dad? Do you?"

"Yes, I do. I feel a lot better—don't you?"

Shawn grinned and nodded. "Now you don't ever have to worry about that."

It was true. The obligation to Mrs. Mendenhall was fulfilled, the debt paid. *Just to clear the slate,* Lois had said, and he thought of her dark hair against the pillow and the way she had looked up at him, something so trusting and earnest transcending the weariness in her eyes that, even now, it made him ache inside. Clearing the slate: he had done it for her, and now he was trying to do it for himself. But there were other things still struggling inside him, other amends yet to be made.

"How would you like to go to St. George?" he suddenly asked Shawn.

"Is it far away?"

"Not really. Forty-five minutes. An hour at the most."

Shawn shrugged. "Whatever. If you want to, I'll go."

Within an hour they had showered and cleaned up at the motel and were speeding along the highway toward St. George. Shawn begged to sing "Daisy, Daisy" and East Side, West Side," but Gavin kept having trouble with the words and found his mind wandering too much to even hum the tunes all the way through.

Zinnie Stokes, Zinnie Gunderson—what did they have to do with him? Whether he pictured the straggly child being chased through the schoolyard or the young widow waiting out the last two months for her baby to be born, the image seemed strange and foreign to him. *Zinnie Stokes, chews and smokes . . .* The whole thing was baffling—incredible. What midsummer night's magic had been played on him? It was as if he were finally beginning to wake from a bizarre, four-day dream in which he had somehow been miraculously dazzled by—of all people—Zinnie Stokes.

What would J. D. say if he told him? He *would* tell him. Or would he? Fifteen or twenty years ago, the words *So-and-so loves Zinnie Stokes*, scrawled on a wall, would have been the ultimate insult, the supreme humiliation. Yet that hurt. The striking young woman in the garden, by the campfire, in the canoe, under the pines—what resemblance did she have to the scrawny little Zinnie Stokes from out of the past?

If he had not awakened from the dream, if he had lost his head totally and decided to take her back with him to Ohio, how would his friends back there have seen her? The Bettridges, for example? Or Katy? Lou and Diane? The Murchisons? Or people from work like Ted and Sheila Walker? But this too made him uneasy, because he knew how they would see her—how could they help but see her any other way than as genuine and radiant as she really was?

So what did it matter if she had once been strange little Zinnie Stokes? Or what did it matter if, twelve years ago, she had run away and married someone like—

But that was what hurt the most, wasn't it? It was hard to imagine, yet Scott was Bryce Gunderson's son. How could he handle that?

They reached St. George at twenty minutes past four, and after getting directions from a bent and spindly service-station attendant and a bulky passerby loaded with groceries, they pulled up in front of Sargent Realty. Before they were even out of the car, Gavin recognized J. D. through the big plate-glass window. It startled him at first, for he could see at once that, although it was unmistakably him, the figure standing there in the loosened tie and rolled shirt sleeves was much heavier, much balder, than he had been prepared for.

He helped Shawn out of the car, then looked over at the window once more just in time to see J. D.'s mouth gape open as he took his hands from his pockets. By the time they reached the door, he was already there, hand outstretched, to greet them.

"Why, you old bounder!" J. D. said, grinning, slapping Gavin on the upper arm as he gripped his hand in a hearty handshake. "Where the heck have you been all these years? Man, it's been ages!"

Gavin could feel his whole body beginning to relax in the midst of J. D.'s enthusiasm. More than once he had tried to envision this reunion—and everything from a formal shaking of hands to an exuberant bear hug had made him uncomfortable. But now, here it was, a vigorous gesture belonging somewhere in the middle, and he realized he couldn't have asked for more.

"It's been a long time," he said, smiling back at J. D.'s wide grin.

"You're not kidding," Sargent retorted. "Why didn't you ever let anyone know where you were?"

He hated the question, but once again he worked his way around it. "Lazy, I guess. But I thought a lot about you guys—about Cedar City and all." He glanced over at Shawn, who had seated himself onto a big vinyl chair just inside the office. "This is my boy, J. D.—Shawn. He's going on seven."

"Hey, big feller—put 'er there," and J. D. thrust out a beefy hand that engulfed Shawn's meekly offered one. "This all? Where's the rest of your brood?"

"That's it," he said with a shrug. "In fact, there's just the two of us now. My wife—my wife, Lois, passed away last winter."

"No kidding! Hey, that's tough. Sorry to hear that. Accident or something?"

He shook his head. "Cancer."

"Oh, no," J. D. said, giving his head a little tilt, as if surveying Gavin in this new light. "Bad news, man. I mean, it really is."

He tried to shift the subject. "But—we're hanging on, aren't we, Shawn? We're going to make it." He glanced around for a place to sit down, just as J. D. picked up a stack of papers from the other chair that matched Shawn's and motioned for him to take it.

"Only one kid, huh?" Sargent started in questioning, seating himself on the edge of a desk, his stomach and thighs bulging inside his clothes. "Man, I've got six already. Oldest one's going to be in junior high in a couple of years."

"Who did you marry, by the way? Anyone I know?"

"Probably not. RaeLynn Heaps from Fillmore. I didn't start dating her until I was student-body president. Here she is," he said, turning a framed eight-by ten colored photograph around on his desk. "Not bad, huh?" A young girl, eyes sparkling and bare shoulders rising from a swath of tulle and taffeta, beamed brightly from a painted blue background. "She still looks pretty much like that," J. D. went on proudly. "She was a cheerleader, Harvest Ball Queen—you know the type I always liked. Hey, man, you've got to come up to the house and meet her. I want you to see our place, too. And I'll take you up on the mountain where we're going to be building next year."

He glanced down at his watch. "We might have to pass on it for now. Maybe we could try to get back down here—"

"Down from where? Hey, man, you've gotta fill me in on everything! Where've you been living? You went east, right? Philadelphia or somewhere?"

"Philadelphia," Gavin nodded, and for the next hour they traded stories, jumping back and forth in time to reconstruct for each other the events of the past thirteen years. Vickie, he learned, had waited for Kevin Sorenson while he was on his mission in Taiwan, and they were now married with three or four kids and living in Denver. Sharilyn had married Royden Anderson from St. George, moved to either Henderson or Las Vegas, separated from him at least once, gone back together, then—

"Hey, Gavin," J. D. suddenly stopped, his face breaking into a wide grin. "That's what you ought to do—take a little run down to Las Vegas and look up Sharilyn!"

Something stirred faintly within him, but he felt uncomfortable with J. D.'s enthusiasm.

"Sure—it'd be perfect! Listen, I saw her a couple of months ago, and she looks great as ever—honest—even after four or five kids. I had lunch with her, in fact, and we shot the breeze. Your name even came up, if I remember right. Hey, what do you say? Want to call her up? Or better still, just run down there. You can get to Vegas in a couple of hours. I don't know her address, but I can tell you exactly where she works."

"Nah," he found himself protesting, "I don't think—"

"Hey, man, it's your big chance. She went back to Anderson a couple of times, but this time the separation's for good."

He could feel J. D. studying him. "What d'ya say?" J. D. went on. "And no Bryce Gunderson to scare you off!" J. D. burst into a deep laugh, then stopped. "Hey, you heard about poor old Bryce, didn't you?"

He nodded. But it wasn't Bryce whose image came before him. Another name, another face, kept rising up in front of him, like a child in school, hand stretched high in the air, begging to be called on. Still deliberating how to bring it up, he suddenly found himself pronouncing the name: "How about Zinnie Stokes?"

There was a second or two of silence. "Zinnie Stokes? You heard about that, too? Can you believe it? Sharilyn jilts him, so he runs off one night and marries, of all people, *Zinnie Stokes!*"

He nodded slightly. "I heard."

"Well, you know he must have been drunk." J. D. laughed. "I sort of felt sorry for poor little old Zinnie, though, actually," he went on. "I mean, she turned out to be not such a bad looker after all, but still—I mean—"

"Have you seen her lately?" Gavin cut in.

"Lately? Nah, I guess it's been ten years or more. Why?"

He shrugged. "I don't know—it's just that—well, I saw her a couple of days ago in Cedar and—" He hesitated, not wanting to meet J. D.'s eyes until he had decided exactly what he wanted to say. Suddenly he looked at him directly. "She's changed, J. D. I couldn't believe it."

"How do you mean? You mean changed for the better?"

He nodded. "She's—she's a beautiful woman, do you know that? You wouldn't—"

J. D.'s mouth dropped, and there were a few seconds of silence. "Are you—are you kidding me? You're not interested in *Zinnie Stokes*, are you?"

He started to speak, but J. D. cut him off, "Hey, come *on*, Gavin, surely you can do better than *that!*"

He could feel himself wince. He took a deep breath and got up. "I'm not sure about that," he said, half aloud.

"Hey, listen to me—what about it? Do you want me to try to get Sharilyn's number for you? I'll tell ya, Gavin, if I was still single—"

"Let me think about it," he said.

"I'll tell you right where she works—"

"Let me think about it," he repeated. He glanced out the window to where his car was parked in the late afternoon sun. "I really ought to be going, I guess."

"Going? Hey, come on. I'd really like to have you see our place."

"Maybe another time—okay?" He held out his hand and tried to manage a smile. J. D. looked at his hand for a moment, then took it in a warm grip. "In any case," he heard himself going on, "I'm glad we got together, for a while at least." And—" he hesitated, taking another deep breath, "I'm glad there seem to be no hard feelings—"

"Hard feelings?" J. D. interrupted.

He managed a little shrug. "About the old days. The election and all," he said.

J. D. seemed surprised. "Not on my part—not at all. But how about—"

"No," he returned quickly, shaking his head. "Not at all. I'm sorry I wasn't a better loser—going away the way I did without saying much. But that's all over."

"It sure is," J. D. said, clasping a big hand on his shoulder as he turned toward the door. Shawn slid from his chair, stuffing the *Star Wars* figures back into his pocket. "Actually," J. D. went on, "being student-body president was no big deal. Well, I mean, it was a big deal, but—well, you actually might turn out to be the big winner, after all—know what I mean?"

Gavin turned back to look at him.

"I mean, I can tell you exactly where Sharilyn works. " J. D. winked at him. "There's a little coffee shop called Benny's. Here." He pulled a calling card from his shirt pocket, turned it over, and quickly scratched out an address and map on the back of it.

"Cream of the crop, I'll tell ya, Gavin," J. D. smiled, tucking the card in Gavin's shirt pocket and giving his upper arm a hearty slap at the same time.

"Thanks, J. D.," he managed, reaching down to take Shawn's hand.

J. D. walked with them to the car where they exchanged addresses, said their good-byes, then parted, J. D. standing on the curb, hands in his pockets, as they drove down the street and turned the corner.

At the intersection of Main Street, Gavin hesitated. Las Vegas *was* less than three hours away. But something gnawed at him to turn east, and he soon found himself on the freeway heading toward Cedar City.

Hey, come on, Gavin, surely you can do better than that! He flinched, but kept his eyes on the highway that seemed to be speeding toward them, then disappearing under the nose of the car. *No, friend,* he wished he had said. *No, I'm afraid not. I'm not sure anyone can ever do better than that.* But even that didn't quite say what he truly wanted to say. All he really knew was that he wanted to be back in Cedar City—now—back at the little house with hollyhocks, and the last golden rays of the sun coming through the trees.

I'll meet you here just about dusk—just about the time the sun goes down, the way it was the first night when I met you out by the fence . . .

All right. Meet me there—where you saw me then . . .

He glanced off to the west. The sun already seemed lower in the sky than he would have imagined. He checked his watch. They would have plenty of time. *Too* much time. He wanted to be there now with the sun already dipping into the horizon.

When he drove up to the house, just after eight o'clock, he felt as excited and nervous as he had when they had driven by it an hour and a half earlier, on their way back from St. George. But this time there was a tinge of anxiety as well, for earlier he had been relieved that she had not been there, somewhere in the yard, to see them as they passed by; now, however, he wanted to see her already standing by the fence or maybe weeding the flowers that grew along the west side.

"You can play here for a while, until it starts to really get dark," he said to Shawn, as he got out of the car.

"Can I play with Scott? Can—"

"Let me check first," he answered. "I'm not even sure they're here."

He stepped across the ditch, pushed open the stubborn little picket gate, and moved quietly toward the house. It looked as surprisingly empty and forlorn as it had all the other times. No worry. Why should he expect her to be there inside? She would still be next door at Gundersons most likely—although a glance back at the road told him her car was not there either. Unless it was around the corner on the other street. He knocked uneasily on the door of the little house, then tried the knob. Locked. But there was no need to worry, he consoled himself. She would come.

He walked around to the side of the house. Try not to look impatient, he told himself, just in case she were watching him from one of the windows next door. He squatted down, feigning an interest in some of the dark pink flowers that still grew against the honey-colored stone. From time to time, he glanced off toward the Gundersons' house, and then, finally remembering the spot where Scott had been sitting on that first evening, he got up, stretched his shoulders, and wandered to the other side of the lot where a dilapidated wicker seat rested in the weeds against a row of lilac bushes. For a long time he sat there, the amber light fading to the lavender-blue of dusk.

It was a quarter to nine when he got up, and hesitating for only a moment in front of the little house, passed through the gate and started toward Gundersons'.

"Weren't they home?" Shawn asked, a touch of anxiety in his voice as he stood up from where he'd been watching his fleet of homemade ships navigating the ditch.

"Not quite sure yet," Gavin said soberly. "Hang on here a few more minutes."

He walked to the wire gate in front of Gundersons', pushed it open, and followed the walk to the big front porch. A light was on inside, and he could hear the sound of a radio or TV coming from somewhere.

He knocked on the door, waited, then knocked once more, a little louder. Someone was coming, but when the door opened, it was a middle-aged lady, wearing glasses, that he didn't recognize.

"Is—is Zin here?"

The woman switched on the porch light and hesitated

for just a moment. "Zin?" Then she began to shake her head slowly. "No, I'm afraid they've gone."

"Gone?" he asked, his voice sounding hoarse.

"Gone back. Back to Logan."

He felt sick. "When—when did they go?"

"Oh, I'm not sure, really. Three or four hours ago, anyway. I guess it must have been about—oh, I guess about four or five this afternoon that they—"

"Are you her sister-in-law?" he cut in.

"Yes," she answered.

"Did she—by any chance—leave a message? For Gavin Terry?"

The woman looked sympathetic, but shrugged a little. "Not that I know of." She gave a helpless little shrug. "I can check, though. Maybe Mama knows something . . ." Her voice trailed off as she disappeared into the interior of the house.

He felt as if someone had just knocked the wind out of him, and he looked off anxiously through the dusky light toward the fence, the poplar trees, and the little empty house next door. Footsteps in the house jarred him, and he realized the woman was coming back to the door. Maybe—

"Nothing," she said, shaking her head and giving him a look as though she were truly sorry. "No one seems to know anything."

So what did it all mean? He glanced nervously out into the waning light. "We all—we all used to go to school together," he found himself explaining. "You're Bryce's sister, I guess."

She nodded.

He swallowed. "We all—Bryce, Zin, and I—we all went to school together here." He wanted to stop the ache inside, but it wouldn't quit. "I just heard about your brother a few days ago—and I'm sorry. I truly am." And as

they stood there in silence on the big porch, he knew it was
true.

"Do you have their address in Logan?" Bryce's sister
suddenly asked.

"No, but—"

"I'll get it for you," she said, and in a moment returned
with a little piece of notepaper. "At least you can write."

He nodded, his mind wandering as he absentmindedly
folded the little paper several times in his hands. "Yeah,"
he said. "I can always write." He looked up at her. "Well—
thanks anyway," he said.

"Sorry you missed them," she told him, and he made a
little helpless motion with his hand and turned away as he
heard her close the door.

He walked down the steps that led from the porch and
then hesitated for a moment on the walk. He had stopped
before like this that first night he had seen her, and he
looked again now, one last time, at the fence that ran
along the east side of the big yard.

He wanted to see her there, her long, pale hair visible
in the near darkness. He wanted—

He stopped. Something white was stuck in the top of
the wooden fence.

He went to it and withdrew it from the little niche
where it had been placed. It was a sealed white envelope,
and on it was marked simply "Gavin."

He opened it and found a single sheet of stationery
folded inside. Unable to make out clearly the neatly hand-
written contents, he walked across the lawn to where the
light from the porch fell across the letter:

Dear Gavin,

I've decided it's best if I don't see you
again, even though I told you last night that I

would meet you here. Forgive me for breaking my promise. I'm sorry.

And I'm sorry about last night—for bringing up more of the past than I ever intended, and for letting myself become emotional. I'd like to think that I have my life more in control than that.

Believe me, I admire your efforts to make amends for the past. All of us, I'm sure, must have things we would like to do over again or make right. But I don't want to think that your interest in Scott and me these past few days is simply some way of unconsciously trying to pay a debt—whether it's to me for that silly dance so long ago, or to Bryce for all the bad feelings you had there. These thoughts have haunted me today. You can't use us to ease away your guilt—I think you understand that.

So consider all debts paid. Please. And forgive us, again, for leaving without a proper goodbye.

Zin

He stood for a long time staring at the page, feeling the oncoming night slowly deepening around him.

Someone, down the street, was practicing the piano once again, and from somewhere else a woman's voice was calling children home to supper. He glanced back at the lonely fence and, for a second, thought he saw a face approaching on the other side.

Whatever it was—the breeze ruffling the vines against the side of the little house or just a mean trick his eyes were playing on him—it was not there when he walked over to the fence and stood there grappling with his emptiness.

"Dad?" he heard a voice call softly.

"What is it?"

"It's getting dark."

"I know," he answered. Too dark, in fact, to even read his watch. Whatever time it was, he strained to see the hands or read the numbers. Las Vegas was really only two or three hours away. And there would even be a time change there, if he remembered right. It would be an hour earlier. He hesitated.

Shawn met him at the Gundersons' gate. "So now what are we going to do, Dad? Do we have to go to bed, or can we—"

"We're going to go," he interrupted. Again he hesitated a moment. "I think we're going to go somewhere."

"Where?" Shawn asked, as he climbed into the car. "To a movie or what?"

"Better than a movie," he said, getting in behind the wheel. He waited for a few seconds. "I think maybe we'll go try to find your friend Scott."

Within half an hour they had packed up at the motel and taken I-15 north. He didn't have the heart to tell Shawn exactly how long the trip would be—seven or eight hours at the least, he figured—but he tried to sing with him instead until the boy quietly curled up against him and slept.

He, too, slept—at a rest stop near American Fork. But by the time the sun was just beginning to lighten the sky beyond the mountains, he was already on his way north again. By eight-thirty he knew that Logan couldn't be far.

He glanced back at Shawn, still asleep where he had transferred him to the back seat, the car blanket having slipped almost totally from his shoulders onto the floor. Shawn would be glad to see Scott again. Maybe it would even be Scott who would answer the phone. *Hey, I've got a little fellow here that doesn't feel quite ready to go back to Ohio without seeing you guys a few more times*, he might start out.

And then what? That would be the hard part. Still, Zin had said something about everything now being even—or something to that effect. And if she really believed that, then the idea of being able to start from scratch, of starting over, exhilarated him.

The sun's rays were coming through the trees now, and the faint mist hovering just above the fields was beginning to dissipate. He opened the wind wing, letting in the cool breeze that smelled of damp grasses and fresh clover.

It was like that first spring day, two or three months before, when they had sped along the highway between Columbus and Cleveland, delivering the book to Mrs. Kocherhans. Clearing the slate, paying the debt.

Consider all debts paid, Zin's note had said, and he wanted to believe now that, finally, it was true. Then what else had she said? Something about not using her or Scott to clear his conscience about the dance—or about the way he had always felt about Bryce. For a moment he tried to force himself to concentrate on the dance: but that was over now, truly over. He had shared his guilt, apologized, and she had forgiven him. So that was finally finished. Erased. Gone.

But Bryce—? Was she right, in any remote sort of way, about his motives there? Was it true that, for him, consciously or unconsciously, the only way to rid himself of the old hatred that had simmered for so long inside him was to see if, somehow, he could try to make it up to Bryce's son?

For a moment his stomach seemed to contract like a tightened fist, but then, almost in the same instant, he became aware of a strangely contradictory sensation: it was a kind of letting go, a steady slackening, as all the tenseness quite unexpectedly eased up, relaxed, and he found himself leaning back against the seat, letting his breath come easy, deep, and slow.

Even Bryce then: that was over now too, wasn't it? The menacing words echoing across a vacant lot so long ago, even the angry warnings murmured in defiance in front of the high school years later—in the end, what did they all mean? And what did they matter? Maybe the old hard knot in his stomach that had always been Bryce Gunderson was now, at last, beginning to loosen—and maybe it was, after all, because of Scott. But not because of any noble sense of duty or because of any debt he felt he still owed that tough-boy whose life had suddenly been cancelled by a senseless car wreck. It was something else— and he longed to explain this to Zin and help her to understand it. The image flickering through his mind split into two conflicting fragments: he could still see the dirty-faced bully with his mongrel dog, shouting his threats across the empty lot on that bleak and cloudy afternoon long ago. But he could also see another boy, quieter, more gentle, sitting alone on a wicker bench near the stone house on that first hushed June evening just a few nights before. And if that boy, big-brothering Shawn along the moonlit lakeshore or through the quaking aspen, was part Bryce Gunderson, then maybe it was not only Zin that was showing through, but also a side of Bryce himself that no one perhaps had ever known or understood.

But there was still something else, and he could feel it now as he had felt it waiting on the big porch of the Gunderson house in the twilight a few hours earlier. Maybe it was too soon to put it all together, yet—just as he had known even while he stood in the doorway talking to the older sister of the dead boy who, not unlike himself, had lost his heart long ago back there in that crepe-paper past to the girl, dressed in blue, dancing in the arms of someone else—he knew that he really did feel sorry, truly sorry, for Bryce Gunderson and for his losses.

He could feel the breeze blowing cool against his cheeks, and, from the back seat, Shawn was yawning. He glanced anxiously ahead, searching among the distant trees and hills for a sign that Logan was not far.

They still had a ways to go. But they were close.